Hidden in the Early Light

~ a tale of the Irish famine ~

By Tecla Emerson

Hidden in the Early Light

© 2021 by Tecla Emerson

ISBN: 978-1737761501

Edited by P.F. Klyce

Cover Design by Katharine Sodergreen
sodergreen@aol.com

Page Design by Robert Henry
http://righthandpublishing.com

Printed in the United State of America
Published by OutLook Publications
Pub3000@aol.com

Dedicated to all those

who came before us . . .

. . . . ONE

"Da! The stink! Come quick." The door slammed behind her, the crash loud in the morning silence. Tossing back her dark braids, she ran the short distance to his bed.

"What Katy," he asked, his voice groggy with sleep, "what are you talking about girl?" He untangled himself from the thin blanket that had been wrapped protectively around him.

"Da, that smell! The one from before. Last year," she said, her breath came in short gasps, "Do you not remember?" There was fear and trembling in her voice. "It's out there Da. Please Da, come quick." She stood next to the straw filled mattress, looking down at her father, her hands twisted in her apron.

Rubbing at the sleep in his eyes he struggled to sit. He slid his legs over the side of the bed, his feet hit the coldness of the dirt floor. The groans told of another fitful night.

"Where's your Ma?" The sleep dimmed his

eyes as he peered into the corners of the room.

"She started early. They've gone to the village. You've got to come Da."

He looked at her, his light blue eyes growing large. "What's that you say?" His voice rose, trying to grasp what he just heard. He reached for the trousers tossed on the back of the chair. Ragged and stained from too many days in the fields, he pulled them on.

"She's gone to the village."

"No girl! About the stink?"

"Da, I told you it's back."

"Oh my God. Help me Mary and Joseph." She expected nothing less. In times of trouble, it was an exclamation he'd always favored. He pushed her aside. "Where? Whose field?" He didn't need an answer. In three strides he was through the door.

"It's in all of them. Look." He stopped and rubbed at his eyes. Together they stood staring across the acres and acres of sloped fields, each section neatly divided by low rock walls.

"Agh Gawwd," he said his stale morning breath further polluting the air. "Agh Gawwd," he said again, as if willing the stench away. His feet carried him to the edge of his yard. It was fenced by a low rock wall, a wall he'd built not so very long ago.

"Where? How?" Work worn hands went up to his face wanting to cover his eyes to shut out what he was seeing. Fingers calloused and bent from age and too many days tending to tidy fields, rubbed at his eyes. He stared in disbelief taking in the endless terrain, his mind not wanting to accept what they were seeing.

She was frightened. Rarely, if ever, had he been so distraught. "The sun came up just an hour ago. It warmed the fields and it started. The smell. It's awful," she said, her voice sounding apologetic.

The air was heavy with the thick, odorous, gaseous stink rising from the fields. It threatened to choke all those who breathed it.

Where's Ma? He's going to lose his mind she thought. Everywhere they looked they saw others spilling out of their homes, their steps reluctant and slow as if in a dream. They made their way toward their fields with slumped shoulders. All had the same look, part anger, part disbelief, part sadness and part terror. Women held their starched white aprons to their noses; men had all manner of rags held to their faces cutting out the dreadful stink hanging over the land. Children frightened by the silence stayed close to their mothers, their small fingers tangled in the long ties of their aprons.

"Da is it...?" she began, her voice no more than a whisper.

"Aye, it 'tis for sure Katy girl." She saw tears in his eyes, a rare thing. In all her years, there had only been once when she could re-member his weeping. It was painful to even re-call – and it wasn't more than two years ago. It was that last babe - but she didn't want to think about that.

"Katy, it is," he said interrupting her thoughts. "We're finished." Hesitant, he stepped through the gate; he knew he'd go no further. He refused to turn in her direction, his eyes riv-eted in horror on the field with its drooping slimy green plants that just yesterday had stood so tall and lush, their bushy stalks reaching for the sun. Turning, head down, he took Katy's hand and as if in search of a safe shelter headed back to their yard.

"But how?" she asked, tears threatening to spill over her dark lashes. "It's already hap-pened once. How can it be again?" As she spoke, she caught sight of her mother and three broth-ers hurrying up the path that separated them from their neighbors. Their feet left no footprints. The path was packed hard from endless years of wear. Her mother's eyes were cast down, her handkerchief held securely over her nose. The boys stayed close, looking everywhere at once, seeing their friends but not daring to raise their hand in greeting.

Mamai pushed open the creaky gate, taking time to close and latch it. The basket of brown eggs that she'd gone off with just an hour ago was still securely tucked under her arm. She said nothing. Her tiny frame crossed to her husband on feet that moved as if they'd been dipped in thick mud. Setting the basket down, careful not to upset the eggs, she slipped an arm through his. Taking a moment to catch her breath she said, almost as a whisper, "I smelled it before we got to the village. We turned around." Her voice was calm, but she shook her head back and forth, disbelief clouding her eyes.

"It's over Tors. We're done for sure." He used the shortened version of Victoria, a nickname he'd made up. In their eighteen years together, he had rarely if ever called her by her proper name. Too Protestant he said for the likes of him.

"We can plant again. There'll be other harvests," she answered quietly, always the voice of reason. Her fingers, in an all too familiar gesture, closed around the locket that hung around her neck. It gave her a peace that nothing else could.

The silence was near deafening. A black crow, its beak blood red against the grey sky cawed madly, piercing the silence as it winged its way over the rotting fields. It was as if his shrill cry gave the women permission to let loose with their wailing and keening.

Katy, her hands hanging by her sides, felt the warm hands of her two younger brothers, Eamon and Conor, as they slid into hers.

"What?" asked Eamon, just above a whisper. At nearly four years old he remembered little of the devastating blight that only last year nearly wiped out the entire crop of potatoes, the most important source of food for most of the Irish.

Kaitlyn held their hands, annoyed slightly by the stickiness of the damp little fingers. She led them into the coolness of the stone house.

"Come along," she said. They looked up at her with wide-eyed adoration. "We'll leave them alone for a bit."

Sean, his mood showing in the hooded eyes and tight frown followed close behind. At fifteen he wasn't quite as tall as his sixteen-year-old sister but was gaining fast.

The latch clicked as she closed the bottom of the split door, the top half left open hoping to catch a breeze.

"Shoo," said Katy, as she flapped her apron at the rooster that had chosen to follow them. He flew up and perched on top of the loom, standing proudly as if it was his and wondering why they were intruding into his territory.

"If Mamai sees you sitting on her loom she'll throw you into the stew pot for sure. Now shoo." He flew through the air, landing on the bottom half of the door flapping his wings in protest. Sean reached over and pushed him back outside. The squawking racket broke the eerie silence.

"Leave him be, Sean," she said, "You don't always have to be so rough." He ignored her.

"It's the blight, isn't it Katy, just like last year," said Conor. His usual cheery face looked angry and hard, and all grown up.

"I think it is. Can't be any other with that stench."

"I saw the plants all bent over," said Sean. "I told Ma that's what it was. She didn't want to believe me." He pushed the long strands of unkempt hair away from his face, revealing a sprinkle of freckles. "Looks just like last year, only this time I think it's got all of them." His voice was mature beyond his years. He thought he was all grownup, but the freckles said differently. Da had said when he was a boy, he'd had the same sprinkling of what he called leprechaun dust. But much like his youth, they were long gone.

"Oh Sean, stop. It may not be that bad. Here you two have some milk. You must be hot." She poured two mugs of the frothy white liquid that Sean had brought in earlier, "And we've some oat cakes left from your breakfast," she said breaking one in half. "Sean, you stay in here now and let Mamai and Da be alone."

"Why do you always have to tell me what to do," he said. It wasn't a question. Turning, his hands balled into tight fists. He stomped out the door. It slammed shut with a crash.

"Oh, fiddle faddle!!" she said shaking her head. "You always do exactly what you want don't you." The two younger boys giggled up at her, their milk mustaches making them look like unshaven old men.

"You always do exactly what you want," mimicked Eamon.

"Oh, hush now," she said pretending to slap

him on his head. "Finish up now, the both of you. There's going to be work to do." And life is going to change forever.

But she didn't say that out loud.

. . . . TWO

The door creaked in protest as it was pushed opened. Three sets of eyes turned in silence to watch as their parents stepped into the room. The two, hand in hand, said nothing but the pain of what they'd seen was etched in deep furrows outlining hooded eyes.

Da spoke first. "Katy girl, get your Ma a cold drink will you now?" His eyes lingered on his first-born taking in the tall straight girl who was so bright and quick and usually so cheerful. He knew she saw everything, missing nothing. At sixteen, she was ahead of her years and was well aware of what was ahead for them. But he knew she would keep her silence. Many a time he'd wondered where this mysterious Irish fairy had come from with her dark brown eyes, so different from the others and her thick dark hair with blonde threads shining through.

"No, no," her Ma protested, "I can tend to myself." She pushed away his hand.

"Here Ma, I have it," she said placing the lukewarm buttermilk in her Mamai's hands.

"Well thank you then," she said, taking a sip.

"And here Da one for you." His pretty daughter placed it in his hands before he could object and patted his arm in reassurance. "It'll be alright," she said wishing that she felt the truth of her words. He seemed to be in a daze, hardly even aware of his family clustered around him.

"We're ruined you know." A thin dribble of milk trickled out of the corner of his mouth. He wiped at it with the back of his hand.

"Now Jamie, you can't say that. We'll be all right; it will all work out for the good." Mamai's voice was soft, but reassuring. "You've fourteen good acres here, we've managed a living before. We can do it again."

"Nay Tors, we can't do it, there's nothing left. We had so little from last year, hardly enough to get through. Now there's nothing. There's no hope."

"Jamie," she said flashing him a look that Katy knew was a warning, "be careful, the children."

The children already knew, thought Katy, there is no hope, so stop trying to protect us. How, she wondered, can they continue on with this year after year of trying to dig out an existence with no end in sight? They'd never have extra. They were always going to live hand to mouth. To be poor. To be potato farmers. That was all her Da knew. She tried to choke back the bitterness that rose in her throat, threatening to choke her. Visions of sailing off to America danced before her eyes. *If only*, she thought.

"I'm sorry Tors," he said turning to his wife, "Tisn't a way we can fix this one."

"And don't we have some of our acreage rented out? We'll be collecting our rents soon enough and then we can pay our rent." There was a lighthearted lilt to her voice.

"And how is it our tenants are to pay their rent? Their potatoes are gone too and then how do they eat this winter? Nay Tors we can't pay our rent," he said rubbing his forehead with a gnarled hand. Grime was etched deep around his fingernails, it told of endless days and months of working the fields.

"I will weave more linen," she said.

He looked as though he wanted to laugh but then thought better of it. "There is no market for linen anymore Tors, you know that." He looked over at the huge loom dominating an entire corner of their small hut.

"Then we'll sell it," said Katy's mother looking too at the huge wooden structure that had meant so much to her. "It's all I have," she said, her voice low, maybe speaking only to herself.

"I know Tors, I know. We almost made a go of it, now didn't we? Now we couldn't even give that monster away."

Katy gasped, but she knew it was true. No one wanted a loom for a skill that few used anymore. She loved it, maybe only because it spoke of a different life or maybe because it was one of the few things from her mother's past.

From the time she was very young, Katy had often spun the crinkly flax into threads that her mother would use to weave into fabric. Her young fingers loved the feel of the fibers as she sat at the spinning wheel, spinning endless strands. She'd done it almost from the time when she'd taken her first steps. But then the demand for linen had gotten less and less and now she spun the threads only when her mother made clothing for their own household.

"And why can't we get the Earl to lower the rent down to where it was?"

Her mother had such a cheery, almost child-like outlook, always so sure everything would work out. Katy turned away, irritated, knowing life was going to be changed forever. Knowing too that she was never going to be free of this place. Knowing there was nothing more to look forward to and that nothing could be done.

"And would you be meaning it will return to where it was before we put the two windows in?" he asked. A corner of his thin lips curled up in a twisted smirk.

Katy would have laughed if the situation hadn't been so dire. They didn't even own the farmhouse they lived in and yet they had made it into a comfortable home with two glass pane windows. It allowed the light to shine in and brighten the insides. But at what expense? The Earl had rewarded them by raising their rent.

"And so why is it now that we can't ask him to lower the rent to where it was even if he says we have to take the windows out," she said.

"And how is it you'll be asking the Earl? My recollection is that we've never even laid eyes on him." His voice began to rise in frustration. "He doesn't even live here. The last time anyone even caught sight of him was months ago. And that was when he was riding in his grand carriage to visit his estate."

"Well and can't I write well enough?" she said. "I'll get a letter to him."

Katy watched her Da as he scowled. He had his days. Often, he would brag of his wife's ability with the written word. She was one of the few that they knew of who had schooling. At other times it made him ashamed that he was unable to read even the simplest things and yet she could.

Today it annoyed him. Katy had seen him this way before; usually it was because he was embarrassed at not being able to provide properly for his beautiful wife Victoria. She had been from "away" and he had wooed her and convinced her to come and live in his village, certain that he could provide for her and create a comfortable life.

"It'll be alright Da," she said not meaning to barge into their conversation, but her mother was tiring, and it would help if her Da would go on about his business and not bother her with his hopelessness. "We can work," she added.

"And how would that be Katy me girl?" His brogue became more pronounced the more upset he became.

"Well, I can go into the village and work at one of the big houses," and never come back she thought to herself. Maybe save enough to leave the farming life forever and head across the seas. "The boys can certainly hire out," she continued, pushing down the thoughts of a different life. A life in a far country. America maybe.

"I'll not hire out any sons of mine," he said.

"You mean Sean?" she asked realizing she spoke too quickly.

"I mean all of them," he said loathe to admit that Sean, his first-born son, his favorite, would never be allowed to work away from home. "T'isn't anything we can do I tell you; we'll all be starving by winter." He slammed his cup down on the table. Milk sloshed in small puddles.

Jumping up, he nearly upset his chair. Ignoring the commotion he was making, he rushed out the door. It slammed behind him.

"Mamai," she said, rushing over to right the fallen chair, "It's going to be alright." But they both knew a fallen chair was a bad omen. Nay, she thought, it will all be fine - as long as I keep doing all the work. She sighed; glad she hadn't said it out loud to upset everyone further.

Looking over at her mother she regretted the unkind thoughts. The dark circles under her once lively sky-blue eyes still hadn't gone away and it had been almost three months since she'd lost that last babe she was carrying. She hadn't gained her health back from the one she'd lost two years before that. How could she have let that happen to herself?

"Here Mamai," she said ignoring the question that had no answer. "Eat some of these oatcakes. They're left from breakfast."

"Nay Kaitlyn, leave them for the boys," she said using her pretty daughter's more formal name.

"Ma, they don't want them. Now go on ahead and eat them or I'm going to feed them to the chickens." She put the two lone oatcakes on a plate and placed it in her mother's hands.

"You boys go on outside and help Da. Go on with you now," she said nearly pushing them out the door. "You eat Ma. I'll tidy up and do some spinning, maybe then we can get the loom going again and do some more weaving."

Her mother had once loved the rhythm of the shuttle as it was thrown back and forth. It seemed to bring her a peace or a contentment when her hands were busy creating a piece of hand-woven cloth. But now rarely did she even touch the loom, often letting the dust accumulate on the once polished frame. Gently Katy pushed her stooped and tired mother into the chair, careful not to upset the plate of oatcakes.

"And look now," said Katy, "there isn't

enough thread left to work the loom anyway. We'll get to that later," she said, hoping to get a response. But her mother ignored Katy's light-hearted chatter.

"I'll do some mending," she answered. "Idle hands are the work of the devil," she said, quoting one of her favorite proverbs. "There's much to be done and I can't very well sit here all day."

"Then here you stitch up the tear in Conor's pants," she said taking the mending basket and placing it within easy reach of her Mamai. "You're a bit pale still Ma. Still not feeling yourself?" she asked as she poured the pail of milk into the churn. Most days her mother annoyed her with her happy face and her cheerfulness always so sure that everything would work out, but today she looked worn. Dark circles were etched beneath her eyes.

"Ah now Katy don't be worrying yourself on my account. I'm fine, just a mite tired is all." She pushed back a wisp of hair. "Started out too early this morning I guess."

Katy was at the churn, pumping the dasher worn smooth from endless years of use. The familiar sound of the up and down motion was soothing. "Well seems like you eat hardly a morsel," she said, "And I hear you at night tossing about when you should be sleeping, and I know Da worries about you."

"Kaitlyn, he just wants to provide for us that's all. Putting food on the table has been getting a wee tough, but it'll get back to rights after a while, you'll see."

"And do you think we'll ever have money or anything Ma? I mean wouldn't it be nice to just once have a new dress or even a good pair of shoes like that silly Elaine Boyle."

A wistful sigh escaped; she didn't need to trouble her mother further, but somehow it all didn't seem fair. They were so poor, they worked so hard and there was never anything left over. She looked down at her own patched and mended dress and saw her dust covered toes peeking out from below the hem. The hem that had been let down so many times and now there was less than half an inch that was turned up. The top was too tight, and the elbows had patches. Stop it she said to herself, this isn't making anything any better.

"Now," said her mother, a false cheeriness in her tone, "You mustn't speak so of our neighbors. Elaine Boyle means well. And for us, well now there've been a few hard years. I'm only sorry that I couldn't bring something to this marriage except that," she said nodding towards the ever-present loom. "I had all that once you know. And more, I suppose." She sighed, not wanting to linger on what might have been. Her fingers closed in a gesture all too familiar, around the heart shaped locket hanging from a chain around her neck. A faraway look like a shadow lingered in her eyes.

Katy stood; she had pounded the dasher long enough. Straining the milk, she let the clotted butter collect and then set it on the sideboard. There had been little to work with, so it had gone much quicker this morning. "I only wish..." she started but then let it go. There was no sense in playing the game of what might have been.

Pulling the small stool to the spinning wheel she sat and willed her fingers to get busy with the threads, wanting to do something so they could stay away from any talk of potatoes and how they were going to manage. "Well now, just look at her," she said, not wanting to end their chatter, about their neighbor. "Look how she flounces herself around with her flaming red hair and she's always so sure to make us all notice whenever she has anything new. Humph," she scowled, spinning the wheel too fast. The long twisted thread broke. Annoyed she picked up the two ends and with little thought her fingers twisted them back together.

"And the only one that's ever noticed," she continued, "is Sean. He's sweet on her you know." With this Katy left her spinning and held out her threadbare skirt and did a little pirouette around the wooden spinning wheel.

"Oh la, aren't I beautiful in my lovely new dress." Her imitation of Elaine Boyle was so close to the real thing. A perfect copy of her mincing ways and slight lisp. Her Mamai had to laugh in spite of herself.

"Oh, stop Kaitlyn, you're too funny. Stop now, this isn't the time to laugh and make fun." But she laughed anyway whether from joy or just a relief from the sorrow that was on them was hard to tell. It had been so long since her Mamai had enjoyed anything that Katy pranced around and exaggerated her neighbor's posture even more.

"I'm Elaine Boyle," she began, the lisp evident in a sing song voice, "and I have all the new pretty dresses even though I'm the homeliest girl in the land."

"Hello." An angered voice cut through the air, "What is going on here?"

Mamai's laugh cut off deep in her throat. Katy whirled around. A bright red flush traveled from her neck up to her cheeks choking back her embarrassment as she stared at the visitor peering in over the half door.

"Good day to you Mrs. Boyle," she gasped, then "Won't you come in?" Feigning politeness, her head held a little too high.

"I saw what you were doing you nasty girl. Y'er all nothing but a jealous bunch of trashy peasants. How dare you mock my daughter like that?"

"I meant no harm," said Katy, her voice a bit too strong, knowing she should appear contrite.

"Mrs. Mullaney, and how is it you could allow such to go on?"

"Now just a moment Mrs. Boyle." Katy's mother rose from her chair. "You've no call to be calling us peasants. I won't have you talking that way..." But her audience was gone. They could hear her as she "harrumphed" her way back down the walk.

"Just because they farm twenty acres more than we do doesn't make them better," Katy grumbled as she crossed her arms over her chest. A scowl pulled down the edges of her mouth. "And that silly Elaine, little 'Miss High and Mighty,' never does a lick of work. All she does all day is put creams on her hands and color on her lips and then struts around showing off."

"Kaitlyn, that was wrong."

"But look at her. She can't even read. She's such a know nothing. Why is it she has so much and there's so little that we have." Tears clouded her vision. Her mother reached out to pat her arm, but Katy jerked it away and stomped across the room. She returned to her spinning and the wobbly three-legged stool.

Each twist of thread brought a new scowl. The quiet whoosh of the wheel as it turned was all that could be heard in the near silence. The rhythmic sound filled the room.

Her mother stood at the open door looking out over the valley. A deep sadness was etched like a carving around her tired eyes. Katy knew it was going to be a long time before she heard laughter again in their once jolly home. Even the two windows appeared cloudy, bringing little light into the shadowy room. The hard packed dirt floor absorbed any light that snuck in through the windows. Feeling sorry for having spoken so harshly she left her spinning to stand next to her mother.

Oh, to be away she thought as she watched

the clouds float off like soft feathers going where they will. She knew not to say it out loud. Pushing back the stray strands of hair that hung in her eyes she tried to imagine life in America, wondering if there was truth to what she'd heard. Were there really bustling cities with carriages pulled by grand horses? Was it true that there were boats that steamed up and down the rivers and shops that had fine dresses for sale and food enough for everyone? Was any of it true? How was it possible? And how can I get there she thought for the thousandth time? To leave all this behind – that was her dream, but she knew to keep it as her secret.

Clouds had begun rolling in, blotting out the morning sun. The wailing and keening voices of the women in the fields had stopped. There was a deep foreboding silence. Her mother returned to her mending.

A black and white magpie coming to rest on the stone wall fluttered its wings and cried out once. It was a haunting sound that cut through the thick stench.

"One is for sadness, two is for joy," she said, hardly realizing she spoke out loud.

The magpie did not call out again, but flew off, his wings making a harsh clacking sound.

Leaning on the half door, Katy felt prickles of fear and trepidation creep up her back. She shivered in the morning warmth.

. . . . THREE

The cold and damp had crept into every corner and crevice of the old stone house. Months had passed since the discovery of the ruined potato crop. This, some said, was the coldest winter ever, certainly the coldest they could remember. The small turf fire with its flickering flames failed to warm even those who pulled their chairs or stools up onto the hearth. They sat so close that the soaked hems of their dresses or pants would send up thin clouds of steam.

"Ma, you know we have no seed potatoes. We need to find something to plant." She tucked the edges of the wool shawl more closely around her Mamai's legs.

"'Tis true," she answered but her thoughts were with the next meal not the spring planting.

"There's little left. A cup of oatmeal and maybe two turnips. This isn't enough," said Katy, knowing well enough that her Mamai was fully aware of how close they were to starving. A tired sigh escaped before she could stop it. "If Da and the boys don't bring us some fish there'll be nothing."

Katy pushed back the stray wisps of hair that had escaped from her once tidy braids. It was not easy to watch her Mamai as so rarely was she discouraged.

"Kaitlyn it will be fine," she said, trying to bring some cheeriness to her reply. "Somehow we'll get through this."

She looked over at her mother, the hollowness in her face was so pronounced that her once lively blue eyes looked as if they'd sunk back into a cavernous void. Her thick dark blonde hair had thinned considerably and was now dull and lifeless with streaks of grey peppered through it.

Katy pushed herself up out of her chair and shuffled across the room. Her eyes, both tired and sad, traveled around what had been their once happy home.

What had happened to their gay household? Once upon a time, not so long ago, they had laughed easily and often. She looked over and saw her Da's fiddle leaning forgotten against the wall, one broken string hung at an awkward angle. It had been such a lively part of their lives. It now did no more than gather dust. She hadn't heard her mother's voice raised in song in months. Everything in the once snug and welcoming home looked tired and shabby. Even the loom that was her mother's prize possession sat forlornly in the corner, a fine coat of dust masking the glossiness of its fine wooden frame.

Mamai had always been so clean and so tidy; everything in their home was spotless. It was important to her to scrub the walls each year no matter if it was needed or not and then after they'd put in the two windows, she'd spent time every day polishing them 'til they sparkled. Now it seemed that there was dust and grime on everything. Not so long ago the hard packed floor had been swept three times a day. Regardless that the chickens and any of the animals were never allowed in the house. "We're not peasants," she would say.

Early in her marriage Mamai had told her husband that she wasn't raised with animals in her home, and she wasn't going to raise her children with animals wandering in and out, no matter how cold it was for the chickens, and the cows, and the sheep. By the time Kaitlyn was born, Jamie, to please his wife, had reluctantly built a shed in the yard. It was attached to the house without actually being a part of it, which satisfied the prim and proper Victoria. It was a home that could be kept tidy and suitable for their children.

Now here they were slowly starving to death. How would they make it through the next few weeks? Where would the seed potatoes come from?

All during the winter they had combed through the fields on their hands and knees. The endless fields that had not so long ago held what had promised to be a bountiful crop. Now they turned up nothing. There were only dried clods of dirt still stinking from the blight. They had used their hands, instead of the long-handled hoe, determined to miss nothing. Row after row in all the old potato fields, each had been carefully sifted through. It was only last month when they'd been lucky in finding a small cache of twenty potatoes deep in the turfy soil, most still edible.

In good times that was what her Da would eat in just one day. Now they made their cache last for a week. They'd already killed the cow. Da feared she'd be stolen in the dark of night by some of the starving people if they continued to keep her outside. She had never been allowed in the house, which was the way of other families. Her milk had gotten to be less and less and finally with no food, she'd weakened and Da had put her down, sharing as was customary the little they could with the neighbors. Mrs. Boyle had been the first to notice that their cow was no longer there. It was a special knack she had of never failing to be aware when one of the neighbors had extra.

"Now Katy, perhaps they're better off than we are but we need to share. They have more little ones then we do to be sure," her mother had admonished her, "and they must be having a hard time."

"But Mamai," Katy had answered, "they have much more than we do, look how they flounce around, and they all have shoes, and they never share. We're always offering them part of whatever we have, and that haughty silly little Elaine can't even say thank you."

"Katy, and did I raise you to be so selfish? Now you go on over and bring those pieces of meat to them and do tell Mrs. Boyle I was asking for her and I'll have you mind your tongue young lady."

The conversation stuck with her, like cow

dung to an old shoe. Why did she have to be the one to bring food to them? But now all of it was gone, even the bones that they'd boiled down almost to nothingness to create a broth that they all had enjoyed. "Here now, look what I have," said her Da bringing her back to the problems at hand. He and the three boys came in the door stomping their feet and clapping their hands together trying to shake off the chill. Eamon quickly snuck into the side of the hearth, closest to the flickering flames of the smoldering turf. He held out his cold little hands to the bit of warmth.

"Step back there Eamon, we don't need to add burns to our list of troubles," said Da. "Here now wife, I've a bit of a dinner for us all." He proudly held out a small grey fish, hardly enough for a meal. "Now isn't this just a good thing? The boys and me pulled this in. Could've caught more I'm sure but we had a fog bank rolling in. Had to get back to the shore before we was lost for sure." His mood was almost jovial.

"Thank you, Jamie, I knew you'd have success. And to you too boys." She pushed herself up from her chair letting the blanket fall to the floor.

"Now Ma, don't be getting up. I'll take it and

fix up a stew for our dinner."

Katy took the fish to the table and awkwardly scraped the scales and gutted the insides. "Yucky," she said, but not too loud. She'd never been particularly fond of cleaning fish. Why, she wondered again, weren't her brothers charged with the gutting and cleaning?

"Eamon, now you go on and get out of there," she said as she pulled him out of his warm little corner in the hearth.

With the help of the metal bar, she swung the black iron kettle out from its place over the turf, its low flame bringing some warmth to the room. The fish was clean, and she dropped it into the simmering water. It was joined by the two pieces of turnip that were close to mush but would add flavor to the almost tasteless stew.

"Won't be long," she said to herself. The two younger boys, exhaustion overtaking them curled up on her straw mattress in the corner. Sean, slouching on the bench stared moodily out the window watching the drizzly rain run in rivulets down the glass.

"How much longer Mamai," he said. "When is it we're going to get some food and get enough to eat?" Leaning on the table, his chin rested in a dirt encrusted hand.

"Now Sean, we've been over this all. We're doing as well as we can. To be sure we're better off than most. We're all still here you know, while most of our neighbors have already moved on." She drew in a tired breath. "Just look, the Kellys are gone, the O'Malleys have left, the Donohues are gone and who knows what happened to the O'Rileys."

"I know, I know," he said his mood darkened even further. "Where to, don't you wonder?"

"No one is sure. They left during the night." He knew this but she continued. "Well, and then some have died too, but thank the heavens, so far we've survived. We at least have something to put on our plates." She coughed, a racking deep cough that shook her entire body.

"Well maybe we should move on too," he said. There was no effort to hide his annoyance.

"And where is it you're thinking we should be going?" asked his Da.

Ignoring the question, Sean continued, "But Ma, it's almost planting time. What're we going to put in the ground this year?"

"We'll think of something, don't despair," she answered. Her back and forth rocking made quiet creaking sounds as it crushed little bits of scattered dirt.

He should be asking Da, thought Katy. Why would her mother have that answer?

"But there's nothing," he said. "We're all finished. There's nothing we can do." His voice started to rise, anger and frustration oozed from every pore. There was no warning. He slammed his fist down and said, "I'm leaving and I'm not coming back."

He stood, looked around the room in fear or maybe disgust and in three strides was out the door. His father watched, his shoulders hunched, confusion clouded his eyes. He made no move to stop him.

"He's right Tors," said Da, his voice low. "We're sunk, there's nothing left. The hunger. It's got all of us. T'isn't a morsel left. We're going to starve. The tenants haven't paid any rent. Most have gone. So how do we pay our rent?" He shook his head in dismay; a look of bewilderment clouded his eyes. With no explanation he stood up slamming his chair back. It crashed to the floor.

Katy and her mother gasped as he stepped over it. He knew it meant bad luck. Ignoring them, he stomped out the door. Somehow, he lacked the strength to actually slam it. A look passed between mother and daughter. It was one of unspoken fear. Is there more bad luck coming? Katy hurried across the room and set the chair upright.

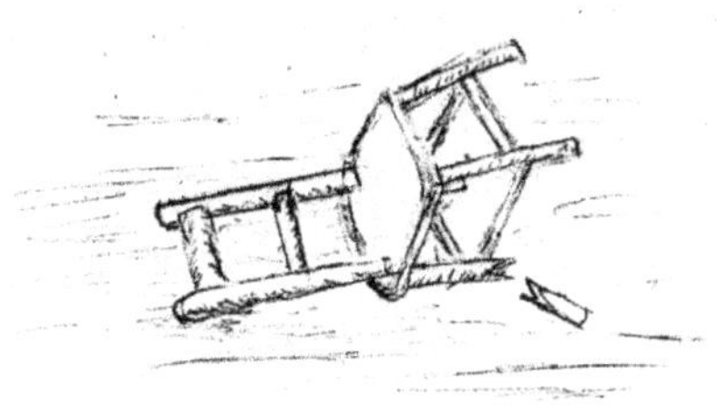

.FOUR

"Ma," said Katy. "What should we do?" She chewed at her lower lip; her eyes searched for answers. They had slept a fitful sleep, reluctant to leave their warm cocoons of ragged blankets. Why get up thought Katy? There's no hope, no food and Da has gone off somewhere.

"I don't know. We must plant. If we don't put something in, we'll starve for sure." Her voice was just above a whisper. She stopped and took a breath. "Katy come over here and sit by me." She patted the blanket on her bed. "I must tell you something."

Katy, reluctant to leave the warmth of her bed, crawled out from under the threadbare blanket. She went to sit where she was told, curious about the seriousness of Mamai's tone. It felt comfortable to be near her and for a moment she took in the familiar scent. It was a mother scent. A scent that only she had. It was warm and homey with a bit of the turf fire and the freshness of outdoors that always seemed to cling to her - and it felt good to be near, inhaling the familiar scent.

"Kaitlyn child," she began, "you know I'm from the mountains over a ways to the north. Well," she said, "there's a story that goes with it that I need for you to know." She covered her mouth with a scrap of once white linen as she coughed a dry cough. Waiting a moment to catch her breath. She continued. Her voice was soft.

"We've never talked much about it but there are things that need telling." Stopping a moment, she gave Katy a long and searching look as if not sure if she wanted to continue. She closed her eyes, her lips moved but no words came out.

As if deciding if she should go on, she waited a moment and then drew in a deep breath. "Your father and I met when he came to our village to sell some vegetables. He saw me one day when I was out at the well." The words tumbled out. "He stopped and said hello. That's where it began. I'm not quite sure why, but from that very first meeting we were sweet on each other."

A smile teased the corners of her mouth in remembrance. "We were married not two months later. There was nothing anyone could do to put a stop to it." She paused a moment to cough again and then cleared her throat. Katy stood. She walked over to the pail to dip out a cup of cool water.

Mamai didn't want to stop. "My parents were Protestants which you know. They were very unhappy with my choice of husband. They told me if I married your Da I didn't ever have to come home again. They made it quite clear they would never allow me back in their home."

She lay perfectly still for a moment, as though exhausted by using up all her words. Her eyes were dull as she gazed out the window into the greyness of the day. More words bubbled up. "My mother was truly sad, probably sad more than angry," Her eyes tried to focus on Katy. "You look a lot like her you know. You're not at all like the others. You have the same blonde streaks running through your hair and the same deep brown eyes. If there wasn't such a resemblance to her, I'd have thought you were a changeling left by the fairies." She smiled a tired smile at her pretty daughter.

It took a moment to catch her breath so she could continue. "Well, my Da was so angry about my wanting to be married, he raged on and on, but Jamie, your Da and I were sure. We would marry. Being a Protestant and your Da a Catholic, the only one who would marry us was the magistrate. So, we ran off without family or friends and were married."

The effort from talking had tired her so that she needed to lay her head back and rest for a time. "Katy, help me up now like a good girl. I've been abed far too long." Was their talk finished? Was this as much as she would say?

Katy pulled back the cover then helped her over to her chair. It was best. Mama was never happy confined to her bed.

The room was dank and dreary with early morning shadows. Her mother shivered. Katy pulled the blanket more closely around her shoulders.

"Well then Ma where is your family now?" Katy asked, her voice gentle, not wanting her to stop, but afraid she was tiring her. She had so many questions like why would anyone leave a life of luxury for a humble hut that they could never even own.

Mamai cleared her throat and then continued, "Well, I'm not really sure where they are now. I did hear from a tinker that was passing through our village that my Da had passed on. He said he was quite sure of it. If it's so, it's sad as I'm quite sure he had no peace." She shook her head as though trying to understand. "He was angry and bitter and at odds with not only me but with the world. The tinker said that my Mamai moved up into the mountains. He said it looked like they had lost everything." She stopped again, taking a sip of the weak tea. Katy had brewed a cup from the leaves that yielded almost nothing having been used too many times, but Mamai didn't complain.

She continued, "My Da had quite a successful linen business. When I was young, I remember how I loved listening to him throw the shuttle back and forth. I couldn't wait until I was old enough to do it. When I left to marry, my Mamai let me take the old loom, the one that she had used all those years. We had to borrow a farm wagon so's we could get it here. It angered my Da even more. But then soon after was when they must have lost everything."

Katy sat by her side and tried to be patient, as each word seemed to be such an effort. But she continued, only more quietly. "The linen business fell to nothing. My Da, I guess, died poor and angry. So, my Mamai, with what little she had, must have left, and gone up into the mountains. I imagine she's still there."

Katy went to stir the bubbling and steaming and not very fragrant gruel. "Kaitlyn, I need to tell you one more thing."

"Yes Ma," she said, sitting herself back down on the wobbly stool.

"I do have something left besides the loom and my locket," she said, fingering the loose chain around her neck. "I have a silver brooch and three silver bracelets that my father gave me for my sixteenth birthday. I wanted to save them for you and your three brothers. Your father knew about all of that, but I think he's forgotten. You need to go and uncover them and take them to town. You can exchange them for seed potatoes. It's all that we have left."

"Where Ma?" she asked, "Where are they?"

Her voice was just above a whisper. "Remember that loose stone over at the edge of the hearth? Slide it out. There's a tin box and you'll find them in there. Please Kaitlyn tell no one. Just take them to the pawnbroker. They're quite valuable really and you should get enough from them so's we can go on."

With that the wooden door burst open. It startled them. "Well Katy do you plan to feed us or sit there and do nothing all the livelong day." Katy, anger wanting to spill over, held it in check. It would serve no purpose. She gave her Mamai's hand a squeeze. A look of understanding passed between them.

"It's coming Da, just a few moments more." She rose and rubbed at the small of her back trying to ease the ache. A reminder that her straw filled mattress was in need of more filling.

"Well, your brother is over at the Boyles, mooning over that red-headed girl, so we'll have one less at the table." Beads of sweat had formed on his forehead. His shirt was disheveled, and a wild look passed over his eyes. He offered no explanation as to where he'd been all night, but it wasn't hard to miss the scent of liquor that surrounded him. It was like a blanket of thick grey fog.

"What is it then Da?" Her anger settled in the pit of her stomach.

"Nothing, nothing Katy girl. Will you be getting us fed or just be standing around talking all day?"

Mind what you're doing she said to herself and with care not to spill a drop, filled the five wood bowls, her stomach growled loudly. The thin pale gruel looked more like water then actual porridge, but it might be the last they'd see for days.

"Eamon and Conor get up and come to the table," she said tipping the pot to get the last few drops from the bottom. "Here Mamai," she said placing the bowl with the largest portion in her mother's lap. If all the angels in heaven were merciful, perhaps it would bring back some of her strength thought Katy.

~

Night settled in too soon, but sleep wouldn't come. The straw pallet was more itchy than usual with pieces of straw sticking through the threadbare mattress cover. It took forever for the boys to settle. Katy stared into the last of the evening embers, waiting for the sound of sleep in their even breathing. There was little warmth from the once cheery flames. Even the hearth with its polished smooth stones looked grey and cold. Sleep threatened to sneak up on her, but thoughts of the loose stone, so close by, kept her from drifting off. She needed to find her Mamai's pieces of jewelry before morning.

What had been no more than a drizzly day had turned into a pouring drenching rain as the darkness of night settled into the snug hut. It rattled the windowpanes and dripped in through the rotted pieces of loose thatch. She needed to get up and put pots under the leaks before it turned the floor into a quagmire of mud. It would be her job in the morning to clean it all up so it would be best to do it now. Maybe it would be a good time to slip the treasure out from its hiding place. Rising up on one elbow she stopped a moment to listen - her father's hushed angered voice cut through the darkness. Had she dosed off? She knew he had gone out, but when had he returned?

"And you know they're going to find me. You know they are."

Katy stopped. Silently she sank back down on her mattress, not wanting to listen to a private conversation. Curiosity kept her from turning away.

"We'll hide you then," whispered her Mamai.

"And how is it you'll be doing that?" he whispered back. "They're going to come and get me. All will be lost."

"But who saw you?"

"It was the Bailiff himself, that's who."

"Jamie, how could you. Didn't you know?"

"And what am I to do? Watch you all starve to death? Is that what you want? Nay, I had to do something. T'isn't much, but enough to buy a bit of food."

"But how? They're going to come and arrest you."

Katy had stopped breathing. What had he done?

"Well now, the Earl had the rents stacked up on the corner of his desk and he wasn't even there. 'Twas the Bailiff that let me in. I told him I needed to see the Earl on a matter of a most extreme importance."

"But Jamie, it's theft," she said trying to choke back an escaping cough. "Isn't a good name better then wealth?" she asked. She knew her Bible verses well.

His laugh strangled in his throat. "I'm thinking it's not exactly wealth that I'm bringing to you now."

The rain picked up in force, blowing hard against the panes of glass blotting out part of what they said. "Jamie, if you're arrested they'll be sending you to Australia, on a prison ship. And how would we ever see you again?"

"I'll go to America, that's what I'll do. I can get to Cork. I'll get on a ship there. There's enough here to do that."

"How could you have done it?" She started to weep. "We've never done anything like that in our lives."

"'Tisn't stealing. Some of that money was mine. 'Twas the rent we had to pay. I only took a little."

"Jamie, it's stealing. We'll lose our house. They'll put us out for sure. We'll lose everything."

"I'll take the money and buy passage to America. There must be enough for that. Aye, and I'll work when I get there. Everyone says there are jobs for anyone who comes," he hissed into the darkness. "And I'll make enough money. Then I can send for you all. In America we'll be able to own land. I've always wanted to own me own land, you know that."

He paused waiting for her response.

There was only a dry, hollow cough for an answer.

"It'd be fine indeed wouldn't it now?"

She could hear her father's smile in his voice, convinced that he'd just solved all their problems. There would be no more troubles.

"Alright Jamie," she sniffed and blew her nose, "but please, now you must leave. If they send the Bailiff for you all will be lost. Go. I'll get your clean shirt and socks. How are we to survive without you?" she said, almost as an afterthought.

"'Tisn't going to be long, a few months at

most and what else is it that we are to do?" The question hung in the air like a late day fog that stayed heavy over the land.

A sob caught in her Mamai's throat. Katy heard her slow footsteps move around the room collecting this and that of her father's things. Her coughing began again. She could hear her Da leading her back to bed and then tucking her Mamai back in. His whispered words were lost in the darkness.

Hardly daring to breath, she pretended sleep but listened as her father crept by. He stopped at the hearth. The darkness was deep. She squinted up her eyes, but the dark was too deep. There were scraping noises. Maybe he was adding more turf to the fire or maybe he was looking for something in the bricks. Katy didn't even want to think.

Listening in the near silence, she heard the latch lift as he slipped out into the rain. The dark swallowed him up as the door closed silently behind him. The sound of quiet was deafening.

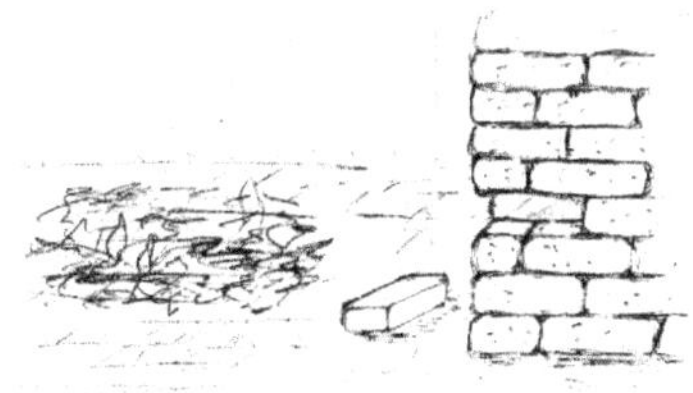

. . . . FIVE

Rain streaked the windows and slipped in under the door. The stone house was filled with a damp and unrelenting cold. Katy lay on her mattress looking up at the thatch. Her Da had meant to repair the leaks last fall but somehow had never gotten to it. There were more drips than ever trickling through the darkened straw. Puddles were forming on the floor. She needed to find another bowl or saucer to catch the drops.

"Kaitlyn," It was her Mamai leaning over her. "Kaitlyn are you awake?"

"Yes Ma. It's alright, I heard."

"Oh Kaitlyn, I'm so sorry."

"It's alright Mamai," she said wanting to believe her own words.

"We'll get the seed potatoes. We'll be alright," her mother said trying hard to sound cheerful. "We just need to get them planted and get through the summer. By then your Da will have sent the money for our trip to America.

You and the boys can fish, and we'll go into the hills for plants. We'll think of something. They say there's Indian meal in the village. We only have to go in and fetch it." She ended with a fit of coughing.

"Here Ma, sit," she said making room for her on the mattress.

"And what, Ma, do we do with the Indian meal?" A bitter tone had snuck into her voice.

"We'll learn how to cook it. If they know what to do with it in America, surely we can learn. It's hard to imagine but that's what they eat over there. We just need to find a way to prepare it."

But how she wondered. It was Indian food that had been sent from the United States of America that was supposed to save the Irish from starvation. But she wasn't quite sure how that was all going to work if they didn't know what to do with it.

Her mother continued. "We have a bit of wool left from the sheep and if we can spin it perhaps, we can trade it for some oats." She spoke with a confidence that Katy knew she didn't really feel. "And next week we'll be celebrating. It'll be St. Patrick's Day and we'll be putting in the potatoes." She was breathless and laid back down next to Katy to rest.

The straw crunched as the young girl rose from the warm hollow she had made in the mattress. Standing for a moment, she tried to stretch the cricks out of her bones. She covered Mamai with the dry part of the blanket and padded silently over to the hearth. With luck, she would be able to prod the embers from last night's fire to get a blaze going for breakfast. Laying two more bricks of turf on the flickering flames she poked at it trying to coax some warmth from it.

A banging on the door cut through the silence, startling her. She hadn't realized how skittish she was. Crossing the room, she ignored the look of fear that passed over her Mamai's face. Taking a deep breath, she lifted the latch. It creaked as she pulled it open.

"Oh, what shall I do," sobbed a distraught Mrs. Boyle. She stood in the grey morning mist; a badly worn handkerchief muffled the wailing. Good heavens. Now what, thought Katy? Not even a greeting, just a sobbing.

"Come in out of the rain," she said, reaching out and taking the arm of the howling and nearly hysterical woman. Raindrops were clinging to her neighbor's unwashed grey hair. "Elaine," she sobbed, "Elaine."

"And what is it? What's happened?" Katy looked over to see Sean rise out of a sound sleep, suddenly alert. He rubbed the sleep out of his eyes.

"What is it?" he asked. Mrs. Boyle sobbed all the louder, choking on words that wouldn't come. Sean crossed the room; he took her by both arms and shook her. "And what is it now?" he demanded, raising his voice. "What's wrong with Elaine?"

"She's gone," she said, gulping air, sobbing, tears coursing down her cheeks.

"And what is it you mean by gone?" asked Sean, his voice rising.

"She's gone. She gone and run off with that no account Jimmy O'Doyle."

"Are you sure?" asked Sean as if he couldn't understand the words. "Why would she do that? Which way did they go? Where are they?"

Mrs. Boyle unable to speak only pointed in the direction of her house. Sean, turning a deep shade of red with hard lines of fury etched in his face, seemed to have lost his speech. Only gasps came out. In three strides he was out the door. His unbuttoned shirt flapped behind him.

"Come," said Katy, "Sit yourself." Gently she led the sobbing woman to the hearth and lowered her into her Da's chair.

"How could she do this," her voice caught, "She knew we needed her. She said it's hopeless she was leaving and that was that. What will become of us?" A fresh torrent of sobbing began. Katy pushed a cup of very weak tea into the woman's trembling hands.

Mamai pushed herself up from the bed and shuffled across the room, a blanket held close, protecting her from the cold. Patting the arm of the crying woman, she spoke quiet words of comfort.

"We can't last," she sobbed. "My Tom is leaving he is. He's to take the two oldest and leave the four young ones with me. He'll send for us he says. Oh, what are we to do. I've lost my Elaine." The weeping continued. It woke the two younger boys who stared wide-eyed, not sure what to do.

"Well, where'd they go? They must have told you something."

Hardly able to sound out the words, she said only that they were getting on a ship.

"But to where?"

"She didn't say." The sobbing got all the louder.

"We'll help now Mrs. Boyle. You're not alone in this. We're all having our troubles. We'll help each other," said her mother as she rubbed at her own belly. Katy watched aghast as her mother rubbed and then patted her belly. Oh no, she thought, it can't be - not another wee one started already. Maybe she's just hungry. But Katy knew that wasn't it and turned away.

~

Sean didn't return for days; and when he did, his mood was sullen. There was a biting anger whenever he was questioned. He had little to say but emptied his pockets of half a dozen turnips, a sack of maize, a small bag of oats and a few very precious seed potatoes.

They didn't ask where he'd been or how he'd acquired the groceries. They accepted it with gratitude shining in their eyes. Glum and quieter than usual they questioned him about life in town. Surely that must have been where he'd been staying.

Katy put a warm cup of what was meant to be tea in his hands and thanked him again for bringing them food. He sniffed a bit at the colored water and tried to appear grateful as he took a sip.

Trying once more to obtain some bit of information about what he'd seen, she sat across from him and waited. Sipping at his tea, even knowing how poor it was, it seemed to relax him. He offered little information; only that a workhouse had been opened.

"People were spilling out of the doors it was so crowded. Four of the more wretched ones were carried out while I stood watching. I don't think they had a breath left in `em."

He spoke quietly almost as if he didn't believe what he was saying.

"There's nearly no food. I stood in line for a bit of gruel. It was awful tasting. Made me sick it did." Unconsciously he rubbed at his stomach.

"You need to boil that Indian meal a long time or t'isn't any good," he said.

Katy had gotten a bowl and was mixing the yellow meal with a bit of water. Why had he returned she wondered? How could what they'd been living on possibly be better than what they had in town?

"And what of the soup kitchen?" she asked, hoping he'd continue talking awhile and not become sullen again.

"Anyone can go," he answered, "But 'tis said it's awful."

"Ma," he said, "there's dead and dying everywhere. There's beggars and wee ones without a

Ma or a Da. There's not a dog left in the village. People are wandering about with no food to eat and nowhere to go," he slammed his fist on the table in frustration as his anger returned.

"You can fish again," said his Mamai trying to turn his thoughts. "You boys and Katy will get the seed potatoes in and then you can fish. We won't starve."

Katy looked over at the sadness etched around her Mamai's eyes.

"We'll be fine," she continued. "Katy, you can go to town with the boys. It can't be that bad."

Katy stood; her fingers toyed with one long braid. And maybe she thought I'll go to one of the big houses to work and then I'm never coming back! I can send them money, but I'll be free.

Daydreaming of the possibilities that lay ahead, a smile played at the corners of her lips. If she could just get away from her family and all the chores and work that was suffocating her... But then felt badly for her uncaring thoughts.

"Ma we'll save what Sean brought us for tomorrow's dinner. I'll go to town and get the Indian meal."

"Nay," she answered, "I'll take the two boys to town Kaitlyn. You've done enough."

"Mamai you can't go to town. You're not well

enough. I'll take them," she said with little enthusiasm. "You stay and rest." She knew even if the walk was fruitless, she needed to get out of the confinement and misery of the house or surely she would go mad. Eyeing the two boys, she wondered if they'd make it. They stood rooted to the spot. Of course, she thought, it's impossible. They're so worn out, they're nearly starving.

"You both stay, I'll go myself."

Once again, she thought if only that brooch and the three bracelets had been there. Earlier, when she removed the brick, they were gone. Even the tin box that was supposed to be there was gone. She knew what happened to them and wondered if they'd ever hear from her father again. It would be too hard to tell Ma and she would of course know who took them.

She picked up the reed basket. It had been woven so many years ago, she hardly remembered doing it. It must have been in another lifetime. It reminded her of happier times. Not so long ago, after the evening meal, they'd knit or weave baskets or do stitching while they gathered around the fireplace. Sometimes Da would play the fiddle. Sometimes they'd all sing. Sometimes Mamai would read to them. Sometimes Da would tell tales of when he was a boy.

His tales were always amusing as he was not above stretching the truth a bit to suit his audience. It all seemed so long ago. Stop, she said to herself. That was then. No point in thinking of what was. Those days are gone.

"I'll be back Ma, I'll see what I can get," she said.

Pulling her shawl over her head she opened the door to the outside world. The air smelled fresh and clean, she inhaled deeply taking in the scent of the emerging spring. The cloying suffocating stench of rotting potatoes had been washed away with the winter rains.

There were a few neighbors left, but not many. The Gradys were still there, just across the way. They'd been busy; there was freshly turned earth. Someone was already putting in a small garden, of what she couldn't imagine. There was so little left.

First, she thought, before I go to town, I'll go and try to get a job at the big house. Surely, they'll hire me. Then I can stay there and maybe there'll be enough to send home. That's it she thought. I'll go to the Earl's. He won't know it was her Da that took the money.

Her step was firm as she set out with a determination she didn't know she had. The drifting clouds held a promise of some afternoon sun. A new, almost forgotten bounce was in her step as she walked in the direction of the big estate. It was a different way from town but one that she could get to and back before the sun set. And it was glorious to walk through the emerging green of the countryside.

Further than she had imagined, she arrived at the mansion footsore and weary. It had been a long two hours. Beads of perspiration dotted her forehead and lined her upper lip. Stopping for a moment she shook out her shawl and tried to smooth the wrinkles from her skirt. Her hair was flying off in all directions and she took a moment to tuck in the escaping curls. Shyness suddenly snuck up on her and doubt crept into her thoughts. She'd never met an Earl before.

The front door was so huge, so imposing, so frightening, she lost the bravado she'd felt earlier. Scurrying down the side walkway she easily found the kitchen door. Hushing the doubt in her mind, she rapped on the smooth wood. There was no answer. She knocked louder. Her knuckles hurt from pounding. When there was still no answer, she made a fist to knock even louder. It was then that the door was thrown open.

"What is it girl?" asked a very tall, formally

dressed man.

Dropping her fist, she stared at the man in front of her. His nose was too large for his long thin face. He sniffed once and looked down at her. "Be gone with you," his bony fingers made shooing motions.

"But Sir, I need to see the Earl."

"The Earl, my dear, does not have time for the likes of you."

"Sir, I come only to offer my services. I can cook and I can clean, and I can read some."

"Go on girl, be off with ya.' We've no need of help from yer kind." The door slammed shut. Katy stood mute. Her feet felt like lead. All thoughts of ever being part of life in the big house floated away.

Where to go now? There were no other big homes that she knew of or that anyone had ever spoken of. Now what was she to do and where could she go? There was nowhere else.

. . . . SIX

Her feet were like lead, tiredness in every limb. The long road ahead stretched without end. There was an ache of sadness that crept into every bone of her body. How would she ever get free? The clouds, hanging back for most of the day, were covering the sky filling the air with a damp mist.

The day with all of its promise was gone. A light drizzle blew through the air. The land-scape all around that had been so bright and promising was dank and dismal in the grayness of the rain.

The devastation left by the long cold winter was everywhere. So many homes abandoned. So many fields grown over with weeds. The trails of smoke curling up from the turf fires in the humble dwellings were few and far between. The silence was eerie. Where once there had been the lowing of a cow and the bleating of sheep kept close by a barking dog - all was gone.

There was nothing.

Nothing. Not a cat or a dog or a goat, not the cluck of a hen, or the cry of a young lamb. There were no barefoot children chasing back and forth between the houses. No Mamai's with their aprons flapping, shooing sheep out of the yard after a child had left the gate open. She was alone. Silence was everywhere. There should have been the smell of freshly turned earth permeating the air. It was that time of year. But instead, there was emptiness all around. And now the dampness once again brought out a hint of the lingering smell of the rotting fields. Maybe so it would never be forgotten?

And there was silence. A feeling of hopelessness lay heavy on the land like a smothering blanket.

A sadness spread over Katy. There would be no pungent smell of the newly spread manure. No scent of the just emerging spring grasses, while the sheep chewed their way through the wild green fields. The scent of mint and garlic crushed under foot at the side of the road was gone. The once homey smell of turf fires was no more. There was nothing. No sounds. No familiar scents. No living thing other than the occasional crow that flew over in its blackness, cawing what may well have been a warning. A warning maybe of more troubles still to come thought Katy.

Slowing her step, her eyes traveled from right to left, trying to find some sign of life, but there were only overgrown, untilled fields dotted with clumps of rush, divided by the ever-present stone walls. The lively green of the bramble bushes along the hedgerows was deceiving. The green hid the prickly thorns. There seemed to be a promise of spring in the air but there was no living creature to celebrate and partake of the new season.

She had set out early. The hope was to find the maize that they were giving out. She had nothing else and couldn't go home empty handed. It was a long walk, longer than she remembered. Much of the day had slipped by when she arrived at the cobblestone square at the center of town. Almost as a warning she could hear the mobs of people groaning and sighing long before she rounded the last corner.

Unprepared for the sight that met her, she gasped as she stepped into the square, her breath catching in her throat. More people than she'd ever imagined were packed tightly together. More even then had ever come to church during holiday time. More than she'd ever seen at one gathering. It was like thousands of ants all scrambling for one dropped crumb of bread.

They were crowded together, pressed against each other, moving as one body, closer and closer to the huge steaming kettles of grey liquid. Not caring what it was they were ladling out from the blackened pots; she joined the throng.

"What is it they're doing?" she asked the scrawny, nearly toothless woman who had pushed her way in front of her.

"Soup," she said, "'tis soup. What're ya blind?"

"Who and from where," asked Katy, ignoring the curt answer. It felt like she was wasting more energy than she had in saying just those few words.

"Quakers no doubt," she growled, "or it might be the Guvn'ment," with this she cackled a strange dry laugh.

"Is it for anyone?" asked Katy. But the woman had turned away. She'd answered enough questions.

The crowd pushed and surged forward. It was going to take what little energy she had left to get to the pots. So many people. There were mothers weeping without sound, sprinkled through the crowd. Some held small children that looked like little sacks of potatoes flung over their shoulders, unmoving, more dead than alive.

Katy felt herself being pushed and carried forward in the crush; at times her feet weren't even touching the ground. The groans and sighs and curses flooded the air. The hot mass of stinking, bony bodies moved her forward. After what must have been hours, she stood at the huge kettle of grey gruel.

Looking into the steaming pot she thought she'd swoon from the heat and from lack of food in her stomach.

Standing in front of the man with the ladle she held out her hands. "Now what would you be thinkin'?" His voice was loud and angry. He picked up a corner of his badly soiled apron and wiped at the perspiration that dripped from every inch of his face. "Where's yer bowl?"

"I have no bowl," she answered.

"Well then be gone with ya'," he said reaching for the bowl of the next in line.

"What do I do?"

"And are you thinkin' it's me who makes the rules?" But he reached under the table and came up with a small teacup. "Here, take this and be gone with ya'," he said. He slopped a ladle of hot liquid into the cracked and chipped cup. It spilled over Katy's shaking hands. She winced at the pain and looked at the meager portion. "A bit more please Sir."

"Nay. Go on with ya' now. You've had yer share. Next time bring yer own bowl."

Holding the steaming liquid close she made her way over to a stone wall, away from the others. Carefully she balanced it so's not to spill a drop. A few steps from the wall a big man, shoeless and grumbling, jostled her.

"Why'nt ya' watch where yer goin'," he spat out at her. She was holding the cup as steadily as possible, but some of the steaming liquid slopped over the sides. Tears came to her eyes as she watched the precious soup spill onto the cobblestones. Fearing loss of more of the hard-earned liquid, she stood where she was and slowly drank it down. She wanted to save some for her family, but her hunger took hold. Not even a drop was left. She would have to return home with nothing.

"There's cornmeal over yonder," she heard someone say as she was jostled yet again. Turning to look she saw another mass of people pushing forward to a table piled with small sacks. Walking slowly, waiting for the goodness of the soup to creep through her bones, she joined the throng willing herself to stay upright and not faint from exhaustion. Once again, she became part of the mass of stinking, scrawny bodies and was pressed forward.

"One only," barked a man with hairy jowls who was handing out the parcels. "Boil it," he said as he handed one to each pair of waiting hands.

"Where did it come from?" asked Katy when she was handed one small sack.

"Why from America of course. Move along now." Katy tucked the small sack deep in her apron pocket and set out to make her way back up the road. Meager as it was, she would have something to bring to her family.

Refreshed a bit from the soup she was more aware of the stink that was in the air. The soft scent of spring was no more. It was the stench of death like a thick suffocating blanket that had settled over the land. What was to become of them she thought as she watched the sun slip slowly behind the mountains?

She continued walking. It was going to be slow, but Mamai would be waiting for her. What would she say? Best to just leave it she thought and not share her tale of going into the countryside to visit the Earl's home.

They were waiting for her as she slipped through the door in the near darkness. She had few answers for Mamai and became withdrawn, choosing to hide in her silence. Mamai said, "We will learn how to cook with this maize. You'll need to go back to town for more."

"Perhaps," she answered.

. . . . SEVEN

Molly was born too early and too small.

"Ma," said Katy, holding the tiny mewling bundle. "What should I do?"

"Ah, Katy, now keep her warm by the fire. There's not much else to be done." She laid her head back down. The effort of speaking had used up what little strength she had. Katy looked at the impossibly small bundle. The baby named Molly stopped her struggles for just a moment and opened her dark blue eyes. She looked up at Katy.

"Oh hello little baby," she said holding her close. "I don't know what's to become of you or what's to become of us, but somehow you've survived being born. Now to see if we can keep some life in you." She put her finger on the nearly transparent tiny hand and watched as the slender fingers curled around her outstretched one.

Earlier, at the neighbor woman's direction,

she had found a wooden box, cleaned it, put straw in the bottom and covered it with a thin piece of linen. The neighbor Mrs. Bronlin was not happy to be brought over to assist with the birthing. Katy didn't know what else to do or who to call and with only two homes still occupied, there was no one else.

Mrs. Bronlin had never been one to keep her opinions to herself and let Katy's mom know exactly what she thought of a woman alone with four children already. Katy had tried hard to redirect her talk from what she thought of Katy's Da, as well as everything else that had been going on. She was not one to be put off and it was a relief when she determined that she had done her bit. She wiped her hands one last time on her stained apron and tried to fluff out her skirt, but it hung in limp and tired folds. Her parting words were clear - the new babe would not survive a day.

Katy had tried to be polite as she opened the door so she could take her leave. It was a relief to wish her a good day and close the door securely behind her.

"There little baby. She's gone. You'll be fine now," she said, lowering her to the bed next to the fire, "You should be warm and snug there."

"Katy let me rest a bit then bring her here and I'll feed her," said Mamai, her voice losing strength. "If only your Da were here. What shall we do Katy?" she whispered.

"It's alright Ma, we'll think of something." She leaned over the hearth and put a handful of oats and a cup of cornmeal into the boiling water, letting it simmer.

"Breakfast soon enough," she said. "This will hold the boys awhile."

They must have heard her because when she looked up the two faces with hollowed out cheeks and huge staring eyes peered at her from their bed.

"It'll be ready in a moment," she said to them, "but first come and meet your new sister." The boys shuffled across the floor; Katy marveled at how they minded since the starving time began. It was as if they had no will left of their own. From the once mischievous and energetic boys they now walked as if in a trance. Sleeping was what they did most often.

The only activity that Katy could get them to do was fishing with Sean. But even he was losing interest. They pulled in fewer, and fewer fish and the last time had brought home seaweed to cook instead of fish. It made a horrible stew.

Katy had gone to town one last time to trade the two very small brass candlestick holders that they hadn't yet sold. Going to the pawnshop before dawn the transaction was completed quickly. It was all that they had left. In trade, she'd gotten a small sack of barley and one of oats; hardly a fair bargain but she had no choice. The barley with a sprinkling of herbs had improved the seaweed stew somewhat.

"You two come sit and I'll give you some oatmeal. It'll be a few moments only."

Together they shuffled across the cold floor. With no objection they took their seats at the table. They had both looked in the direction of the box that had held the tiny infant, but they had no questions. Conor, unable to hold his head up, laid his forehead on his arms, his breathing coming in shallow gasps. Katy tried to ignore the quiet sounds of discomfort around her. She thought she'd go mad if she continued to listen to the cries of pain and suffering, or worse, dying. It had been all through the neighborhood and now even in her own home.

Humming an old tune under her breath she tried to blot out the noises that echoed through the house and tried to ignore the rumblings in her own stomach. She stirred the porridge and continued to hum, every now and again looking into the old wood box holding the now wakeful infant.

"How did this happen?" she said to the tiny babe. "How could you be born into such as this?" She reached out a hand to tuck the rag of a blanket more closely around her.

"Molly, that's what we're to call you, Mamai said. Said she wanted to call you Mary, but she'd already lost one babe named Mary. So, Molly it t'is." Her voice was barely above a whisper as she rubbed a finger along the baby's nearly fleshless arm. Her skin, more white than pink, was wrinkled like that of a wizened old woman. "You're not the most beautiful thing I've ever seen, but we'll try to keep you with us as long as we can. It would be nice to have a wee little sister instead of all these boys, and you have such pretty blue eyes. Am I really to be the only brown eyed one in this whole family?"

She smiled as she stooped down next to the box. She very much wanted to curl up on the floor tucked next to the tiny babe and fall into an endless sleep.

Tiredness had seeped into her every bone; she didn't know how she could go on another minute. Maybe it's time to give up she thought.

Maybe I've tried long enough. It's not possible to keep ahead of the demands of this starving household. All I want to do is go away. Away from all the misery and starvation. If only I could, she thought.

There had to be a better way, she just knew it, far from the drudgery and monotony and the poverty, away from the constant needs of family and the dependence on crops. But where could she go? I'll think about this later she said, but not aloud. Something will come. America! But she pushed it from her mind.

"Eamon, get back, you're too close to the fire. I'll serve you in a minute." She stood, her hands reaching around to rub the soreness in her back, "I'll be back in a moment," she said, "I need to get some air."

Stepping outside she breathed deeply of the warm air. The sky was sparkling blue but there would be rain before long she was sure of it. Storm clouds had been gathering on the horizon. A light breeze cooled the dampness that clung to her hair.

Tiredness seeped into her every bone. She stood a moment looking up at the heavens, "how much more?" she asked, "how much more can I do?"

One lone tear trailed down a grimy cheek as she looked over at the few leaves of the sparse potato crop. She swiped at the tear with her once clean apron and breathed in more of the warmth of the air. "How can we make it? How are we to survive?" she whispered into the breeze. It seemed to be calling to her almost as if urging her on. To where she thought. If only I could go into the hills and wander by myself for a while to get away, away from all this.

A high-pitched scream sliced the silence of the bright morning. A shiver ran up her back. "Oh no," she said as if already knowing what had happened.

"Eamon," she screamed as she tore back through the door. His screams filled the little house, bouncing off the cold hard walls and filling the smoke-filled space beneath the thatched roof. In two steps she was at his side.

"What is it," said her Mamai, lifting herself from the mattress.

Eamon sat on the hard floor holding his wrist; not daring to touch his hand, his mouth wide open wanting more screams to come out but there was nothing but a choking sound. He looked imploringly, pleadingly at Katy and then fell back, fainting dead away.

"Gawwwd," she said, not caring if she cursed. She could hear, more than see, her Mamai falling back on the mattress. Conor was standing at her side and Sean as if woken from the dead sat bolt upright in his bed. Ignoring them all she picked up Eamon's burned hand, "Why did you do that," she said to the now silent little boy. Tears flooded her eyes. "I was going to serve you in just a moment."

Oatmeal and cornmeal still steaming clung to his scrawny hand. It was already turning bright red with blisters forming around the blobs of hot porridge.

"You knew it was hot," she said, tears in her eyes. She lifted him up, surprised at how weightless he'd become and carried him to the table. His head lolled, almost lifeless, his breathing shallow.

"Get me water Conor." Her ten-year-old brother moved as quickly as he once had, surprising Katy with his swiftness, "and a rag," she said. There was nothing else to put on it. There was certainly no mutton fat; a favorite of her Mamai's to rub on burns. There was no chamomile or egg white or mare's urine; there was nothing anywhere to treat it with.

"Cabbage leaves," gasped her Mamai from

her bed. "You must wrap each finger with a cabbage leaf."

"And where would we be getting cabbage leaves?" She hadn't meant to sound so callous.

"You must wrap each finger individually," said Mamai, her words slow and painful.

"But how Mamai. There's no time." She wiped at the tears threatening to blind her. Carefully, gingerly she wiped at the small hand, trying to ease out the pieces of grain that wanted to stick to the young flesh.

"There now," she said as he began to come around. Wrapping the hand as tightly as possible, she used the only piece of linen in the house. "Eamon," she said, not meaning to be quite so cross, "if you'd just waited a moment."

"I was hungry," he began to wail, "it hurts, it hurts." He began to sob and curled up into a ball on the table.

"Keep it still," she said, "and it won't be so bad." But he began to retch, horrible sounds coming from a stomach that couldn't remember when it had last been filled up.

"Here now," she said, faintness nearly overtaking her. She picked him up and walked over to her Mamai's chair next to the fireplace. Together they rocked, tiny pieces of grit made haunting noises as the chair moved back and forth.

"Ah," she gasped and jumped out of the chair. "The oatmeal." It was burning, stuck to the bottom of the old black pot. She took the hook and pulled out the crane, hopefully to save some of it. Eamon now balanced on her hip, wept silently.

Katy wiped the perspiration drops from her forehead and tried to cuddle her young brother for just a moment, then tucked him in next to Mamai. The baby began her mewling cry. Katy tried to soothe her with quiet words, then tucked her into the crook of her Mamai's other arm.

"I'll bring you oatmeal in just a moment Mamai." She turned, tiredness showing in her every move, she tried to straighten her shoulders as she walked back to the hearth, but they didn't seem to want to straighten anymore.

"Kaitlyn," her Mamai said, "come sit by me we'll eat in a bit, while the two are sleeping." Katy sank down on the small three-legged stool pulled up close to her bed. If only she could put her head down on her Mamai's chest and sob. Sob out all the frustration, the anger, the hunger, the hopelessness, but then looked at her Mamai lying flat on the bed. Baby Molly was curled up in the crook of her arm. Eamon was safely tucked into her other side. There was no room for her.

"Aye Mamai," she said quietly, not wanting to waken the two sleeping little ones.

"Here now my beautiful brown eyed child. Sit next to me for just awhile." Her voice was sad. "You know your hair always smells like fresh mown hay; it reminds me so of when I was young." Her hand lingered as she smoothed down the wayward ends that had sprung free from Katy's long braids.

"Kaitlyn, my time here is done, my work is finished." Her voice wasn't much above a whisper.

"Ma don't talk so. You just need good food and rest; you'll be right as rain in no time."

"Nay child, I won't. This birth wasn't right. I can feel it, something's very wrong."

"Ma, we'll get a doctor."

"Oh Kaitlyn, how? Doctors won't travel to our poor area." Her eyes were closed and her breathing shallow. "Death, my child, is the poor man's physician. T'isn't a thing can be done to stop it."

"Ma, please don't talk like that. Da will be sending the tickets soon. We can all go to America."

"Child, it's been over six months. I don't think we'll be seeing any tickets to America," she said.

"But Mrs. Boyle said it can take almost three months just to get there."

"Aye, and that's true enough," she said, "but somehow I don't think I'll be going to America." Her eyes closed for just a moment as though willing back the pain and tiredness that was in every bone of her body. It was many minutes before she spoke again.

Kaitlyn thought maybe she'd fallen asleep and stood, trying to tiptoe away. But then she spoke. "I know that farming is not for you, my child. I can see it in your eyes, how much you loathe most of what we do, but it has fed us, and it has provided a living for us. Katy, all the work you've done, it's all part of who you are and who you will become." Her eyes focused with sadness on her eldest child. "You cannot erase all the sorrow that has happened or any of your past. Why not hold on to what has been and turn it into good?" She stopped long enough to catch her breath.

"Mamai," she said, "Please rest." What she was saying was confusing. How could nearly starving to death serve anyone's future?

"Do you remember my telling you about my Mamai?" she asked, her voice not much more than a whisper, her eyes still closed.

"Aye, I do Ma, I remember."

"Well Katy my child, it may be the way out. My Mamai and Da left the town where I grew up. I'd told you they had a linen business there, but it slowly died away." Her speech seemed to flow more smoothly with her eyes closed.

"She went up into the mountains. That tinker who came through the village months ago had said that. He told me that she lives somewhere up on Mount Carrantuohill." A great sigh escaped. "She was so unhappy with me. She doesn't want to see me. Your Da she said, brought me down and as many times as I've tried to write to her, each letter was returned."

The baby began to make little wakeful sounds. Kaitlyn gently rubbed at her arm settling her down.

"Mamai," she said, barely above a whisper, as though she didn't really want to be heard. "I can't do this. I can't keep on. I don't know what to do or where to go or how to help anyone. I can't do this." Tears were close to the surface.

Her Mamai reached over to pat her hand. "Katy, I'm sorry, all of this has fallen on you.

You're too young to have so much left to you." A tear slid out from under her closed eyes and trailed down into her thin greying hair.

"Child," she said, "you can do whatever you set out to do. Don't forget that. You have the strength. You have more strength than any of us. Don't ever give up." She coughed but went on, her voice tight and strained. "You will survive." A smile wanted to break through the tiredness.

"Katlyn, do you remember how your Da would toss a potato fresh from the fire from one hand to the other when it was too hot to handle? Remember that?" she asked, smiling to herself lost in her own memories.

"I remember," said her eldest daughter, "And then he never dropped it no matter how difficult it was to handle. Even when his hands got burned." She smiled with her own set of memories. "Maybe that's a little like life. We're tossed back and forth with one thing after another." She seemed almost breathless but kept on. "We try to keep from crashing though sometimes we get burned – maybe even have scars. Our troubles are tossed back and forth like that, but we can't give up. With luck and strength, we won't fail."

They both knew that if the potato fell to the ground it would explode in a million hot pieces. She took a shallow breath, "Kaitlyn, I loved him you know."

"I know Mamai, I know," she patted her arm in an effort to ease her pain.

"Your GrandMamai will take you in, I know she will. I want you to find her. She'll help you. I know how much you dislike farming and the potato fields." Her voice wasn't much more than a whisper.

"She'll help you and the others to start a new life. Kaitlyn keep them safe. I'm trusting you. Keep the family together. Promise me Kaitlyn." For a moment her eyes focused on her eldest child. "You look so much like her when she was a young girl. Take the locket, you'll see. There's a likeness in there of her. Go up to the mountains and find her. Here," she said, her fingers pulling at the chain. "Give her this locket and she'll know it's you." She said no more.

Katy could hear the even breathing as her Mamai slipped into a deep sleep. She reached over and undid the clasp of the chain that Mamai always guarded so closely. Opening the silver clip, a sketch of a pretty young girl stared out at her. Is that what I look like she wondered? It'd been quite some time since she'd peered into a looking glass. No doubt she'd changed some since the last time she'd seen herself. She'd gotten taller, she knew that much and from the fit of her skirt gotten much thinner. But the girl in the locket couldn't possibly look like her; the sketch in the locket was too pretty.

"But I can't do this." she whispered to the sleeping woman. "You can't leave me. How will we survive?" But there was no response.

She put the chain around her own neck and closed the clasp securely.

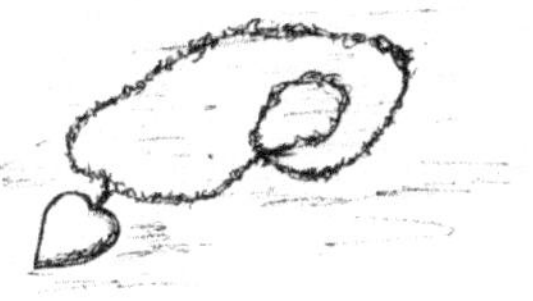

. . . . EIGHT

Katy passed the slane to Sean. "Here," she said, "You've got to help dig. There's not a whit of strength left in me."

Sean's glance was icy. There was an argument in him, but he chose not to pursue it. Taking the pointed digger from her dirt encrusted hands; with a slow and deliberate reluctance he dug out the last few shovelfuls of dirt.

Katy pushed the escaping damp hair back from her face and lifted her apron, swiping once more at the drops of sweat. Her dark brown eyes darted into every corner, taking in everything; the dreariness of the day, the vacant huts abandoned these many months, the lone black crow sitting in the branch of the tree eyeing her, and the vacant landscape where nothing moved.

She felt rooted to the spot. Arms hanging at her side, the last bit of strength long gone, she found herself staring into the bottom of the shallow hole. Puddles began to form from the falling rain. It was cold and unwelcoming. Drips from the naked branches of the apple tree, her Mamai's pride and joy, slid unnoticed down her back.

Katy remembered how she hated it when Mamai would make everyone come out and admire that tree when the fragrant blossoms burst forth in their soft colors early in the spring. It seemed like such foolishness at the time. And now if she could only hear her Mamai's happy voice again. The tree had gotten larger each year to her mother's delight, and often produced a bountiful crop of small hard red apples. But not this year thought Katy, no, not this year when we needed it most.

"Here Katy, that's deep enough now." He leaned the digger against the trunk of the tree. They didn't even have a spade or a shovel anymore. All they had was the slane that they had used when they went down to the bog to dig turf. The turf was all they had to build the cook fire and it was their only source of heat on cold winter mornings.

She wanted to laugh, there was nothing left. They'd sold the shovel, the spade, the hoe, even the cart that they'd used to haul the turf. They'd sold their buckets and rake and even some of the fireplace implements. Most of their cooking things were gone, leaving only four bowls and two pots. There was almost nothing left. They'd let go of nearly all that they'd ever owned. Whatever they'd once had was gone. They'd used every possession they had to barter for grain or food. Even the two chickens were gone. She and Sean had butchered them when their egg laying had stopped.

"Someone will steal them for sure," Sean had said. "We're better off getting them in the stew pot and eating them now." They had tried to keep them in the house for a few days, but their squawking and their mess was so distasteful to their mother that they'd decided it was time; they would make a nice dinner for the family.

They knew they were luckier than most, they at least had meat for a while. The stews and soups and broths that Katy had made from the sinewy meat and bones of the old hens was what had kept her Mamai alive she was quite sure.

But now there was nothing and baby Molly was so tiny, she was probably starving to death. If she was to survive, they were going to have to think of something soon.

Katy looked over at the bare branches of the apple tree. Even it had yielded nothing. It had meant so much to her mother. She loved telling the story of how Da had gone out and dug up a sapling for her shortly after they'd been married. She'd never asked where he'd found it. But Mamai had said they'd always had an apple tree in their yard when she was a child and it reminded her so of home. Her Da never regretted planting it and always took special care to be sure it thrived. It had brought such joy to her mother.

"I'll get her," said Sean bringing her back to the task at hand. "Go get the others."

Together they walked into the house. It was draped in a deafening silence. Sean, head down paying little attention to what was around him, went to the bed and lifted the bundle wrapped in the linen shroud. He walked back out into the cold looming twilight carrying his burden.

Katy came out, a young boy on each side. Conor on the left and Eamon on the right, his good hand tucked safely into hers. What am I going to do about his hand she thought, knowing there was almost nothing that could be done about his fused together fingers. She let the thought drift off.

Mamai had said leave it wrapped tightly for a few weeks; it would keep out the infection. But of course, she had also said to wrap each finger by itself. Katy had been in such a rush that she had just wound the linen scrap around and around his injured hand. Later when she unwrapped it, she was stunned with what had happened. The healing flesh had all grown together. His fingers were welded permanently into the form of a mitten. He had cried, big gulping sobs. There wasn't a way to hide it from him. Later, she'd said to herself. There's got to be some way to cure this. I'll think of something. But not now - later.

Sean clung to the bundle, reluctant to set it down. Katy stood and watched, unable to form the words she wanted to say. Tears threatened to spill over as she watched Sean whispering unintelligible words to the body wrapped in the shroud. A shroud made of the sheet that she had been sleeping on. Sleeping on maybe for all the days of her married life.

She let her mind wander as the cold dripping rain mingled with the tears. Once we had a goat, two goats actually she thought, we had sheep, we had a cow, we had chickens, we farmed fourteen acres of land, we had cottiers who paid us rent each year on the acres that they farmed. We had a dog, we had food on the table. We had potatoes, lots of potatoes, enough for every meal. Da would easily eat twenty at a time each dipped in buttermilk the way he liked them. He could peel a potato with his thumbnail, faster and more deftly than anyone in the entire neighborhood. We were happy. We were a family. What has happened? Why now is there nothing? She wanted to wail in despair.

Sean stooped down, holding the misshapen bundle with unusual gentleness. His knees were getting soaked and dirty from kneeling in the mud. He laid the form in the bottom of the muddy hole. He stood a moment and looked into the depths of the cold and unwelcoming pit; rain coursed down his hollow cheeks.

"Ashes to ashes," he said. Katy loosened the grip of the small hands clinging tightly to hers.

"Say goodbye," she said as gently as she was able. The two stood wide-eyed, not understanding, but managing a tearful "goodbye Mamai."

"And what about Da?" asked Conor.

"And what about him?" asked Katy, a hard-edge snuck into her voice.

"Shouldn't he be knowing?"

"And how would that be?" she asked. Conor

heard the warning in her voice and left it, after all it had been over a half year, and they'd heard nothing.

"Alright now get back into the house and out of the wet or you'll catch your death," she said, instantly wishing she'd used a better choice of words. She watched as the two returned to the house, their bare feet leaving small footprints, quickly disappearing in the soft mud.

"Sean," she said, "I'll take care of it, you go in with the other two." He didn't object. She picked up the slane and threw in one muddy pile of earth after another, getting more and more vigorous with each shovelful.

"Why?" she kept mumbling. "Why Mamai? Why has this happened? Will we always be hungry? Will this ever end?" She wiped at her eyes with the back of a mud-streaked hand. "Mamai why have you left us? What are we to do now?"

Tears, mixed with the early evening rain, slid unnoticed down her cheeks, reddened from the chill in the air. The earth became heavier and heavier as she tossed one rain-soaked shovelful after another into the hole.

Mounding the last few scoops, she threw the

slane letting it clatter against the stone wall. She sat down with a plop on the mound of freshly piled earth. Putting her face in her hands, she sobbed, deep gut-wrenching cries. And then there was nothing left.

From sadness came the anger that boiled up from deep inside. Balling up her fist she pounded the bare mound of dirt and cried out, "We will survive."

The icy wind blasted down from the north, driving the cold rain through the air, soaking her through to the skin. Raising her muddied fist she shrieked out, "I will find a way. We will get through this. I promise you."

. . . . NINE

Molly was not doing well. Anyone could see that. They were going to have to find a bottle to feed her with and then a source of milk. Where? How? There were no neighbors. Maybe in town she thought. Maybe there'd be more maize and perhaps a bottle. Dribbling bits of food between her hungry lips was not going to keep the babe from starving.

It was just after the sun's rays had first shot over the horizon when she slipped out. She had no answers and didn't believe there would be anything at all for any of them, but very early she closed the door silently behind her. She would see what she could see and carry back whatever she could find.

Sean would stay and be in charge. He would surely get into mischief if he was sent out to find what they needed.

As she went along the path, her stomach growling in protest, she found her temper starting to rise. With each step she became angrier, the thought of all the starvation and misery was eating away at her brain - her brain famished from lack of nourishment. With little thought she found herself turning toward the Earl's estate, where she had visited not so long ago.

Her feet took her down the now familiar road. Paying little attention, she nearly tripped over the pile of rags in the grassy mound in the center of the road.

"Food Ma'am," said a voice from the pile of rags.

It was impossible to understand what she was seeing. This could not be. "What has happened?" she breathed out, "I had no idea."

"Please Ma'am," it said

This can't be a human, she thought. It's one of those trolls come out from the forest. She looked more closely. A very thin young girl was holding out a hand that was shaking and was so bony it looked skeletal.

"Who are you?" she asked, stooping down to be on its level.

A murmur passed through her lips.

"Oh, my Lord," said Katy, shocked into silence.

Her answer couldn't be understood, but she

knew this person. Green stains surrounded her once apple red lips. The body of bones groaned, and half opened her eyes.

"What's happened to you?" she gasped. Could this really be? Deep silence surrounded them. Their voices were just above a whisper.

It was Elaine Boyle. How had she been able to recognize her. This near scarecrow more closely resembled a skeleton than their bubbly young neighbor.

"And where is Jimmy O'Doyle," Katy asked, "Your Mama told us you had gone off together." Too late she thought, that was a foolish question.

"Gone," was all the skeletal body could manage. Two front teeth were missing – her lisp was more pronounced. Large sad eyes looked at her, too large for the skull they were sunken into. Dull eyes stared at her, almost no life left in them. It was hard to know if she even recognized Katy.

"Are you sure?" she asked in a voice just above a whisper. The skeleton pointed over to the mud hut set well back from the road. It appeared to have partially melted away in the winter rains. "I'll go see," she said. "You wait here."

But of course, there was no need to say that. There was no strength to go anywhere. The skeleton stayed curled around itself in the middle of the road. Her ragged, too big clothes were spread out around her in a smudged pool of grey.

Katy walked down the littered path toward the windowless mud hut. The creaky gate hung on one hinge. A stench met her before she even crossed the threshold. She lifted her apron to cover her nose and pushed open the door that hung at an awkward angle. Her empty stomach did a flip-flop.

In the corner, just barely visible in the morning light, was what looked like a sleeping person. Whoever it was had a blanket pulled up and was lying on a pile of spoiled straw. It was a man of undermined age, thin as a fence post, stretched out full length, his eyes stared straight up at nothing, his mouth open, one lone fly buzzing in and out at will. Tears came to Katy's eyes; outrage was replaced by horror and disbelief.

"How can this be?" Backing out of the hut, she held her apron tightly over her nose and mouth, leaving barely enough room to breathe. Stumbling back down the path she went out to the road in search of Elaine. She was right where she'd left her lying in the road. The rags that may once have been a new pretty frock, blended in with the dirt.

"And Elaine now we need to get you help." she said hardly expecting an answer. "Come now," she said, "We need to get you out of the road, a cart may come along and not see you and run you over." She was unable to respond, instead only her lashes fluttered. "I'll help you now," she said, "Come along."

She bent and lifted the nearly weightless body. The effort was minimal but starved and weakened it felt like she was hauling a huge boulder to the side of the road. Trying to be gentle she laid her on a sparse patch of grass.

"Elaine," she said, "listen to me now. I'm going to the Earl's house and then to town. I will try to find some food and bring it back to you. Do you understand?" Her eyelashes fluttered like a passing butterfly. Her body, lying on its side, curled back into a fetal position.

"I'll be back, you stay here." As if she could get up and go anywhere, she thought. Looking closely, she noticed the green stains on her lips and chin. She'd been eating grass, or leaves, no doubt. There had been talk that children had been doing that when every other source of food had been exhausted. Maybe it's not such a bad idea she thought as she stood, waiting for just a moment for the wooziness to pass.

It was miles to the Earl's and if she then wanted to go to town, she would need all the strength she could muster. Slowly, putting one foot in front of the other she made her way down the long dirt road past the vacant farmhouses, past the empty fields, through the heavy silence.

No dogs barked, no children played, no farmers were whistling in their fields, no women called out to each other as they shook out last night's bed linen. All was silent.

It was the Earl. He was the one who was responsible. He was the one who kept them all poor and in poverty. He was why they were all starving to death. No one could pay the rents he was demanding. No one had food. There was no money. How were they to survive?

Her pace had quickened, and she arrived much sooner than she expected. With little thought of what she was doing, she found herself standing at the huge door of the grand, almost castle like house. This time she would not go to the servant's entrance. She pounded her fist against the great door. After many minutes with her hand feeling bruised and near bleeding, the door was slowly opened.

"I want to see the Earl," she said with more force than she thought she had.

"You again," said the big man with the long nose.

Taking that for a no she said, "Well I'll just go and find him myself." Ducking under his arm, it was easy enough to slip past him. Chances were that the Earl was in London, his real home, but she had to try. It was said that only rarely did he come out to visit his other homes in the Irish countryside.

"Now see here."

"Where is he?" she nearly screamed.

"May I help you?" asked a large figure. His pudgy pink hand was dabbing at his lips with a snowy white linen napkin. It was a man of un-determined age. He stood in front of her, quite obviously coming out of his dining room. He could only be described as portly, with a round stomach and round face and not particularly tall. He smoothed the ends of his mustache with his thick fingers. "What is it, Robert?" he asked.

"Sir, this girl was here earlier looking for work and now here she is back again."

"Sir, if you are the Earl, tell me this. Why are so many of us starving to death? Why aren't you helping the people? Why do you insist on our paying rents when there's not a halfpenny left?" Tears of anger threatened to spill down her cheeks.

"Have you gone out there? Have you seen the death and wreck of everyone's lives? Why don't you help them?"

"And how is it that you think I can help?" He dabbed again at the last crumbs sticking to his neatly trimmed mustache.

"You could give the people food; you could stop collecting the rents."

"But good heavens girl, then how would I survive? I didn't create the potato blight you know and if your people don't pay their rents how am I to go on? Robert show her out," he said turning abruptly on his heel.

"No. You can't do that. We're starving to death. You have to help us."

"Robert," was all he said as he indicated with his hand that this annoyance standing in his front hall was to be removed.

The tall butler with the overly large nose picked her up by the elbows, took her through the front door and deposited her on the front step. Her foot caught on the brickwork - she tumbled down the stairs, her ankle twisting painfully.

Rubbing at the bruise, she tried to calm the anger that was enveloping her, clouding her thinking. The Earl's land stretched out in endless fenced fields before her. Horses were nibbling at the occasional tufts of grass, enjoying the balminess of the day. It had the look of complete peace and tranquility.

How can this be she thought? With a boldness she didn't know she had, she walked or marched towards the barn. It was the one that held the sheep. Their familiar bleating drifted through the air. A limp from the bruised ankle slowed her progress, but a determination carried her forward.

Slipping through the side entrance she stood a moment, her eyes adjusting to the dimness of the huge interior. There were pens and stalls on both sides. Some held a few sheep that looked at her in curiosity. It took only a moment before she saw a nursing bottle used for the lambs. Most barns had one, as the mother sometimes didn't survive the birthing process. It was then up to the herder or caretaker to find a way to keep the little lamb from starving.

The tin nipple was dented and scratched but it would have to do. It was tucked up on a shelf just out of her reach but easy enough to bring the ladder over to retrieve it. And sure enough the caretaker saw her.

"Whater' ya' doin' up there," he said. The pitchfork that he had been using was pointing towards her.

"The Earl told me he wanted this for one of the pups," she answered, surprised by the quickness of her excuse. Trying not to look guilty or rushed she came back down the ladder.

"I told him there'd be one in the barn." Eyeing him she wondered if she could outrun him, quickly deciding that she had the advantage by being slender and much younger. She held the bottle close and scurried out the door.

"Hey," he yelled after her, "I never seen you before. Where'd ya think yer goin'?" But she was gone. Down the path and quick as a sprite she disappeared behind the hedgerow. Her ankle throbbed from where she'd twisted it, but she had a bottle for Molly. Holding it close, she knew it was going to be a long journey home.

Keeping to the sides of the road and turning now and again to see if she was being followed, she walked, but mostly ran towards home. It was going to be a ways.

She had nearly forgotten Elaine but then realized she was passing the huts that she had seen earlier. She called out, but not very loud: "Elaine," and looked to see if she could find her. Watching closely as she made her way down the lane, she was not to be found. There seemed to be a slight indent in the weeds where she thought she had left her when she pulled her out of the way, but she wasn't there.

A silence covered the land. It was near deafening.

. . . . TEN

"There's nothing left. Look for yourself." He believed her. It was just that he was hoping it wasn't true.

"Sean if you'd taken better care of the boat at least you could be out catching fish." She hadn't meant to sound quite so harsh.

"It was stolen, and you know it," he answered. "It wasn't ours to begin with and there was nowhere that we could hide it. It wasn't my fault. Besides seems even the fish are gone."

"Well, they're not. You just have to find a way to catch them," she said tightening her apron. It was soiled and threadbare like everything else, but it was all she had, that and the ill-fitting dress she wore. Clutching the broom as if it was her grip on sanity, she continued sweeping the imaginary dirt from the floor. "Now what am I supposed to do." The words came out before she could stop them. As if in answer to her thoughts there was a loud banging on her door. This can't be good. There's no one about. We have no neighbors. Maybe we can pretend we didn't hear it. Her feet dragged as she crossed the room. The hair on the back of her neck prickled a warning; she really didn't want to know what was on the other side of the door.

The knocking had turned into impatient pounding. Ignore it she thought and go on with the sweeping. But it wasn't going to go away. With little curiosity, she lifted the latch and in near silence opened the door, her broom clutched tightly in her hand.

"Yes," she said, squinting out into the drizzly, cold, February afternoon. "What is it?" she asked looking out at a burly man. A sheaf of papers was clutched tightly in his hand.

"I'm looking for James Mullaney," his voice boomed. Why do officials always look so official she thought? It took a moment, but she recognized him. It was the Bailiff. The few times that they had been late with the rent he'd come calling.

"Well and so are we," she said, "but he's not here." She would share as little information as possible, thankful only that he wasn't looking for her and the stolen lamb's bottle.

"Then where is he pray tell girl?" Spittle

sprayed out from puffy chapped lips.

"He's not here," she said again, hoping that her answer would satisfy him.

"Well, you need to find him. The rent is far overdue and either he pays it by tonight or yer all out."

"But" began Katy, "how is it that you think he can pay it? Have you no eyes? You have no tenants and if you did, they have nothing and can't pay their rents. And why do you think we could pay ours?"

"Not my problem girl. We've given all of you much too much time to pay up. Now, it's either by sunset tonight or yer out."

"You can't do that. We have a baby, and where is it now that you think we'd be going?" Her knuckles turned white as she clutched the broom. Her eyes shot sparks.

"Can't help if you've gotten yourself with a wee one now can I. That's not my problem. My problem is collecting the rent. Now, you've got 'til nightfall," he said waving his collection of papers, "and then I want you out."

Katy felt a heat rising, starting in the very soles of her feet; it crawled up her legs, through the bones of her back, piercing her shoulders and was red hot when it hit her cheeks. Broom in hand, she had heard more then she needed to. Without a thought in her head as to consequences, she gripped the straw broom and struck out at the balding, perspiring man, hitting him on the head and the shoulders.

"You get out of here," she shrieked, "You get out of here now."

She had little strength left, but she smacked him across the back then hit him on the side of the head. The broom, the wood handle worn smooth from having swept the floor so many times, broke with a loud crack across the Bailiff's arm. The one that held the papers.

"I'll have you arrested you little trollop," he yelled. She hit him again. This time on his retreating backside.

"I'll see you in the gaol. They'll lock you up," he shouted holding the sheaf of papers over his head trying to prevent the rain of blows that crashed down on him, threating to crack open his skull.

"I'll call the magistrate," he yelled. And she hit him again. He tried to duck the blows as he ran slipping and sliding down the walk through the mud and muck. "You'll be arrested, you know," he screeched back at her. He turned and tried to hold her off waving the pile of papers in the air.

"You get yourself out of my yard and don't you ever be setting foot near this house again," she screamed at him.

"T'isn't your house, you little wretch."

She heard giggling behind her but didn't turn, then watched as one after another of mud balls rained down on the fleeing figure.

"You heard her," screamed Conor, "Get your sorry self out of our yard and don't you ever come back."

Sean came running out, the slane clutched tightly in his hands, its sharp metal edge glinted in the light. He sprinted to the edge of the yard to take one last poke at the retreating figure. He slashed once, opening a huge tear in the Bailiff's trousers.

"No Sean," said Katy bringing her broken broom down on the wooden handle knocking it from his hands. "You can't be killing him."

Sean turned; his eyes filled with hatred. "I'm going to Katy."

"Nay Sean, you're not."

The sound of the screaming threats cut through the air as the Bailiff ran down the road. One hand holding together the seat of his pants.

"It's enough trouble we're in," she said to her brother.

Confusion stared out from four sets of eyes. Dirty, hungry, exhausted, poor beyond description, those eyes showed no secret promise for the future. Then in the quiet, holding his web like injured hand to cover his mouth, Eamon started to giggle.

Words of reprimand caught in Katy's throat. Their situation was hopeless, how could he? And then she too, unable to hold it back let a giggle slip out. With that the other two, thinking Katy and Eamon had lost what little sense they had left, started to snicker. At first there was only the sound of unused and rusty giggles and then with no thought to circumstances, the chuckling came. It took hold of them as laughter spilled out so hard and so long, they had to hold their sides for fear they'd split wide open. Tears slid down their cheeks.

"Did you not see him run?" one choked out.

"And did you see the terror in his eyes?" said the other.

"And did you see the rip in his trousers?" giggled Conor.

"And did you see his naked arse?" said Eamon. Katy gasped, then let it go. Eamon at only four already knew far more than a boy his age should ever know.

The rain, the cold and the darkness enveloped them, but the laughter started up again. They laughed themselves into exhaustion. Each time their eyes met the laughter bubbled up again. There was no stopping it. Conor and Eamon with mud dripping off their hands and Katy with her broken broom felt a strange and comfortable warmth.

There'd be time tomorrow to cry she thought, for now this was the best medicine there was.

~

"Sean," she whispered into the blackness, "You have to wake up." There wasn't a hint of light, not from the now cold hearth or the still sleeping sun. "He'll be back for sure. They'll throw us out and maybe put us in jail. No one hits the Bailiff and gets away with it and what if he knows it was me that went to the Earl's and stole the bottle? And Sean, there's no food left." Her breath came in gasps.

"There's nothing in the cupboard. We've used everything. There're no more seed potatoes for the planting, no money and nothing left to sell or trade. We've got no fire 'cause we're out of the peat. How is it then that we'll even keep warm?" He didn't have the answers, she knew that but who else was there?

In the darkness she could hear him throw back the blanket. "Well and then what should we do? There are five of us. Where can we go?" Tiredness, anger and hopelessness was all she could hear in his voice.

"I'm thinking there's only one way. You all go to the workhouse where they'll at least give you food and maybe a job."

"But then what about you and..." he hesitated a moment, "Are you thinking that Molly will make it?"

No one could know if Molly was going to be with them much longer. She slept most of the time, she rarely cried, there was a dull look to her eyes, and her little tummy was swollen and extended. She was most often listless and rarely interested in anything that went on around her. They tried to feed her with the tin bottle, but it was most times only water.

"I don't know. I don't know what to do. There's no food left that's all I know."

"Then where can we go?" he asked.

"We've got to go away," she answered. "If the Bailiff sees us, we'll be punished for sure."

"You'll be safe in town," she said. "He'd have

a hard time arresting a boy charged with taking care of three young children."

"And what about you?" he asked.

"I'll go to the only place that's left," she said. "I'll go up into the mountains."

"But how will you survive?" His feet hit the floor and she heard rather than saw as he pulled the blanket around his shoulders.

The mountains. That was it. She would go and find help. GrandMamai was up there somewhere. Surely, she'd be able to find her and surely, she'd want to help the children of her only daughter.

. . . . ELEVEN

"We'll find her," said Katy. There was no other answer. "GrandMamai is up on Mount Carrauntoohil somewhere. Mamai said so." Pausing a moment, doubt clouded her eyes, but she went on. "Conor and Eamon don't have the strength left to go very far and they'll be needing you to watch over them. I can make it if I go alone."

"I don't know," said Sean, "What if you can't find her? What if she doesn't want you? And what if we're arrested when we get to town?"

"Well then Sean we can stay right here." She leaned over and gently picked up Molly. She cuddled her a moment then held the lamb's nursing bottle to her lips hoping she'd take in some of the water. "There little baby, you'll be fine soon enough," she crooned. The tiny little bundle started to cry; weak tearless sobs that somehow sounded too old for someone so young.

"She's starving to death you know." Her

tone was matter of fact. There was no emotion. She laid her back in the wooden box.

"Alright then, we'll do it. I don't know of any other way. We'd best go before the sun comes up," he said.

"Wake up Conor." She leaned over him, her fingers digging into his shoulder, "quickly now," she added. "We need to go while it's still dark." He lay perfectly still, his breathing even.

"No," he said, "I can't, I'm too tired."

"Conor, the Bailiff may be back. We've got to go now." He rolled over bumping into Eamon.

"Go 'way," said the four-year-old. "Leave me be."

"Now you two, you've got to get up now."

"Why," yawned Eamon. He rubbed at the sleep in his eyes. "Where are we going?"

"You boys are going to the workhouse. I'm going up into the mountains to find Grand-Mamai." Her fingers reached up and for a moment closed around the silver locket.

"Katy, we can't, we have to stay here. What if Da returns?"

"He'll find us, don't worry." As if he was ever coming back! But she knew not to say that out loud. "Come along now, we have to start walking."

Well now here's an interesting thing about owning almost nothing, thought Katy, you can just walk out and shut the door. And they had next to nothing. She picked up the one linen sheet that they still owned. It was ripped and soiled but she took it off the bed and made a comfortable sling for Molly. It cradled her and held her securely bound to Katy's chest. She barely whimpered when Katy picked her up and gave her a few more sips of water.

"We should go now, come along," she said. With a last look back, she bid farewell to her home and to the loom still dominating the room. It sat like a giant ghost in the corner as if it was a reminder of how life had been. It was all that was left. She had tried to sell it but there was no interest. Now it sat in the corner, the only thing that remained in the room. The only piece of evidence that once not so long ago it had been a busy and happy home, where they were able to care for themselves. How quickly life had changed. Someday she wanted to say, I will be back, but she let the thought disappear into the darkness.

Together in the quiet of the fading dark, the four children and one very small baby began their journey down the long, hard packed dirt road, trudging single file through the silence and chill of the early morning.

Sean was sullen, saying little. Katy said nothing as they passed the field where she had so recently tried to help Elaine. The imprint was there in the dirt and tufts of grass where she had curled up earlier. But she was no more.

"Elaine," she had called over and over that day when she had returned from town. "Where are you?" There had been no answer. She was gone. To where she couldn't imagine. Katy had sat next to where the imprint was as she looked in all directions trying to find a trail or something to indicate that she'd been there. There was nothing, no sign she'd ever even existed.

Sean would never know. He'd been so upset when Mrs. Boyle had announced she had run away. He did not need to hear what Katy had seen!

The sun was a ways over the horizon as they arrived in the nearly deserted town.

"It's over there," said Katy, pointing to a dark stone building. It had been the town government building, or so they'd said. It now served only to house the starving masses of people. Many of the once fine windows were broken, the gaping holes patched with paper and cardboard. They could smell it and hear it before they even set foot on the granite staircase. The hard stone was worn smooth by the many feet that had climbed up to the entrance. A few men and boys were already coming out of the building dragging their tired rag covered bodies off, no doubt in search of work.

"C'mon, we've got to go in," she said, giving Conor a shove in the direction of the massive doors. "It's alright," she said pulling Eamon along, "come on now."

She clutched Molly closer to her as they made their way up the stairs and through the wide double doors. Katy searched for someone in charge. Everyone seemed to be in their own world absorbed in their own problems.

There were far too many children who were too small to be left uncared for. They were lined up along the walls in awkward positions, lying or sitting or leaning against the cold stone, some of the littlest ones digging at the chipping paint and eating it. There was almost no conversation, only occasional moans and quiet weeping. Women were bent over; shoulders rounded, eyes blank, trying to see nothing.

Katy hugged Molly closer, trying to block out some of the dank sour odors of too many unwashed bodies. She wanted to flee, but flee to what? They were reduced to nothing. There wasn't a thing left. But was this better then starving?

Turning abruptly, she made her decision; this was not a place where she could leave her family. Focused on nothing but getting out of the stinking building, as fast as possible, she nearly collided with a woman in an apron starched to board like stiffness. It covered a faded skirt that hung in tired folds.

"May I help you?"

"No," said Katy, "we were just leaving."

"I beg your pardon," she said adjusting the pince-nez at the end of a sharp nose.

"There's been a mistake," she said trying to get around the tall bony woman. Stepping around her she walked with determination towards the only way out she could find. The two massive doors opened before her. Katy could see out into the overcast morning and there standing at the bottom of the stairs was the Bailiff. Gasping in disbelief, she turned back to the cavernous hall hoping he hadn't seen her.

"Aye," she said to the tall angular woman who stood watching her. "We need places here for the four children." Trying to stay calm, her voice was breathless in its near panic. If the Bailiff saw them, surely they'd be punished – even put in jail!

"I'm sorry," she said, her clipped English accent enunciating every word, "but as you can see there's really no room." She waved her hand indicating all the bodies spread out on the floor and those sitting on the stairs or just leaning against the wall. Then why Katy wondered did you ask if you could help me?

"We have over twice the amount that we're supposed to have. So go along," she said, shooing them with her bony fingers, much like Katy shooed the chickens.

"But you must. Is this not a government sponsored workhouse?"

"Child," she said, frost dripping from her every word, "do not tell me what I must and must not do. There is no room."

"Well, Miss Finch, is it?" asked Katy, trying to look at the prominent nametag on the chest of the bosomless woman. "We were sent here by the Bailiff," she said, keeping her fingers crossed, hoping that she'd know Bailiff Driscoll.

"He said to ask for you and that you would find places for us." Katy tried to pull back her lips to form a smile but feared it looked more like a grimace.

"He said we'd be sure to recognize you as you were the tall pretty lady with the blue eyes." Katy crossed her fingers more tightly; sure it would forgive the lie that she was telling. She continued with what she hoped was a smile.

"Oh, did he now," she said, an involuntary blush creeping up her neck and into her bony cheeks. She patted her hair pulling a few stray wisps into place.

"Aye, that he did," said Katy. "It was just last night, he said you'd be here, and he was right, here you are." She tried a bigger smile. "The boys don't need beds; they just need to be fed."

"And what will you be doing?" she asked eyeing her suspiciously.

"I need to try to locate someone to help us."

"But you can't just leave your baby here," she said sniffing her long thin nose.

"It's not my baby," she said. "She's my sister."

"Of course," said Miss Finch, her eyebrows raised.

"I will be back to get them all."

"There is no one here to tend to that baby. One of you will have to tend to it."

Katy looked over at her three brothers. Already the youngest two were sitting on the floor, trying to find a comfortable position, eyes half closed. Sean, totally disinterested stood next to the door leaning against the wall looking for all the world as though he were about to fall over.

"We need something to eat. Could we please just have a little something for now? The boys are so hungry, and the baby hasn't had anything except water for two days."

"Well," she said, her thin lips pulled back to reveal a row of discolored teeth, "we'll be having breakfast eventually so you may wait if you choose to. Hmmm," she said, "so the Bailiff really said that." She wandered off, straightening her blouse and smiling quietly to herself.

Katy breathed a great sigh of relief. She repositioned the quiet baby and wandered through the cavernous building taking in all the sights and sounds, the high ceilings, the cold stonework along the walls, the cracked windows and chipping paint. There were few beds. There was no place for a baby and there was no one caring for the small children. How can I leave them here she thought?

Sitting on the bottom of the cold, hard worn stairs she rested a moment. She hadn't eaten in days and would not be able to walk out of town, never mind up a mountain, if she didn't have something soon.

There was no one to help. Everyone was in distress. There were people lying about, too sick to move. On some of the beds there were as many as six children all huddled together. The floors had probably never been cleaned. All sorts of human waste was piled up deep in the corners. Many of the windows had been broken out, some covered with only a piece of brown paper. The windows that still had glass were so filthy and grimy that little light came through. She realized then that Molly could not be left.

Hoisting her into a more comfortable place in her sling she headed to the soup kitchen. "You're staying with me," she said to the sleeping child.

. . . . .TWELVE

They'd been fed. Certainly not their fill, but enough so they wouldn't be sick from the sudden load of foodstuff on their starved stomachs. Katy had heard that many had died unnecessarily from filling themselves full after not having eaten for a long while.

Earlier, with much pushing and shoving, they'd arrived at the front of the mass of humanity. Katy had managed to come away with two cups of buttermilk and a bowl of steaming oatmeal, flecks of yellow Indian cornmeal floated in the jelly like mess.

They found an out-of-the-way corner where they wouldn't be stepped on and carefully shared the little they had. It was a long process spooning bit after bit into Molly's hungry mouth but enough had been gotten into her to stop the sad whimpering. It was easier to spoon some into the bottle that was half filled with watery buttermilk and shake it all together. So soon it was all gone. They needed more. Watching to the left and to the right, she walked over and around the bodies scattered about, determined to find some other source of food.

The kitchen with its half-closed door was right in front of them. For just a moment she stopped to look at the busyness going on in the crowded room with its pots and stoves. Transfixed she watched as workers poured oatmeal and Indian cornmeal into a huge, blackened pot of boiling water. Obviously, it wasn't all ending up in the pot as one worker after another filled small sacks with the grain then stuck them inside their shirts. Was it any wonder the kitchen help was so much more robust than the other residents? If there was a way to stop it, she didn't know how. Without thinking, she slipped through the door.

"Here, here," said a booming voice, "Get on with ya, now. What is it yer doing here? Get out of the kitchen. Ya don't belong here."

The slovenly man, his buttons threatening to pop started towards her, his huge wooden stirring paddle raised in the air as if to strike her. "Get on with ye' now." But Katy had found her prize. He could chase after her all he wanted but she was quicker. Darting between the great kettles, she slipped out the door clutching the overflowing bowl of oatmeal.

Disappearing in the crowd with her bowl of oatmeal, she took a quick visit to the dining hall to empty the few pitchers still sitting about with drops left of buttermilk. They paid her no mind. Everyone too concerned with their own problems. Hiding her bowl of oatmeal in the sling, she gathered the others and together they sat at a table in a quiet corner and shared what they had.

"I'll be on my way soon," she said. The three boys hardly noticed that she spoke. They sat together on the rough-hewn bench all somewhat satisfied from the small offering of food.

"You'll need to watch out for each other now and stay together. Sean, try to get a job in the kitchen, that way you'll find more food. Conor," she said turning to her middle brother, "you watch out for Eamon, and Eamon you try to stay out of the way." She eyed his hand once more. He was so ashamed and self-conscious of his welded together fingers that Katy had to ignore it.

It had been her fault; she was sure of that. It had never healed properly. All the new flesh on the badly burned hand had caused the fingers to grow together. If only she hadn't kept it bound in a rag for so long. There was nothing else to do and she knew only that it had to be kept clean.

It was hard not to relive the horror when they unwrapped the bandage and saw his poor little fingers fused together like a misshapen pink mitten. But now at least it appeared to be well healed. There were no signs of infection. She gave her littlest brother a hug. "I shall miss you terribly Eamon. Please take care of yourself. I'll be back before you even know I've been gone."

"Here Katy," said Conor, "I've a bit of biscuit and there's a drop or two of buttermilk left for Molly's bottle."

"Are you sure you want to take her?" asked Sean, looking over at his sister.

"There's nothing else to be done with her," she said. "I can't leave her here. Who'd care for her?"

"I could," said Eamon.

"Aye, no doubt you could," she said smiling at her youngest brother, "But you need to take care of yourself more than anyone else. She'll be fine. Somehow we'll survive." She took only a sip of her buttermilk then poured what was left along with Conor's share into the baby's bottle.

Molly whimpered softly; she'd enjoyed the

two teaspoons of dripping gruel that Katy had given her. But there would be nothing else for a while as she hadn't eaten in so long it would make her sick to fill her tummy all at once. She'd had to admonish the boys to slow down and eat just a little, taking time to digest before they ate more.

"I must go," she said, hugging Conor and giving Sean what she hoped was a confident look.

Standing, she hoisted baby Molly into the linen sling and snuggled her down as she took her leave. "I will be back," she said, "have no doubt of that. Wait for me. It may take some time." She turned abruptly and walked out, tears trailed silently down her cheeks, dripping onto the cradled baby.

Looking straight ahead, ignoring the pain around her, the sickness, the starving and the infirm, she fled down the stairs, glad only that the Bailiff was no longer to be seen.

The Post Office stood to one side as she made her way along the cobblestone street. Not sure if it would be worth the effort, she climbed the wide stone stairway. Perhaps there was a letter. It was worth a try.

"Mullaney's of County Kerry?" said the

postman, more as a statement then a question. "Nay don't think so," disinterest oozed from his hawkish face. Nevertheless, he pushed his chair back and walked over to the slots holding an assortment of envelopes.

"James Mullaney," she said.

"Don't see anything," he said, as he picked up one after another of the pile. "Nothing here," he said dismissing her with a wave of his bony hand.

She lowered her head and turned to walk away. "Wait," he said. "This looks like it says Mullaney. Looks like the address is kind of worn off. Looks as if it's been here awhile. Hmmm," he said. "Just says Mullaney, not James Mullaney. But 'spose that must be what you're in search of." He turned it over and examined the back. "Looks like it mighta' come from America."

Katy reached out and grabbed at the letter without so much as a thank you. He growled behind her something about ungrateful brats. Ignoring him she rushed down the steps wanting to get far away from town. If the Bailiff was still lurking about, coming face to face with him would be a disaster.

Trying to disappear within the mass of people, she moved quickly, weaving through the throng of bodies. Her feet took her away from the direction of what had been her home for all these years. A moment of uncertainty clutched at her heart. Don't look back she told herself, that's not where you're going. Looking off in the distance she focused on her destination, the summit of Mt. Carrauntoohil.

If she walked for what was left of the day, she might make it halfway to the base of the great mountain. She slowed her pace, no need to rush. Already she was far enough from town so she would be safe from the Bailiff.

Tired and hungry she stopped by the side of the road, climbed over the rock wall and made herself comfortable in the field. She needed to feed Molly again but for now she had to read the letter with the unrecognizable handwriting.

The envelope opened easily; a single written page fell out.

"*DEAR FAMBLY*," it began, Katy thought for one quick moment how glad she was that her mother insisted they all learn to read and write. But if this was from her Da, how had he managed it?

I AM IN NEW YORK CITY. I AM LOOKING
FOR WORK. I HAVE SMALL JOBS BUT I
TRY TO FIND SOMETHING MORE. A LOT
OF SIGNS SAY <u>IRISH NEED NOT APPLY</u>. IT
IS HARD TO FIND WORK. THE RAILROAD
WILL BE HIRING SOON AND THEN I WILL GO
WEST AND HAVE A REAL JOB. I WILL THEN
HAVE MONEY TO BUY TICKETS FOR ALL
TO COME TO AMERICA. I MISS YOU. I
HOPE THAT YOU WILL JOIN ME SOON. I
HAVE A NEW FREND HIS NAME IS SAM AND
HE WRITES THIS FOR ME.

SIGNED,
YER LOVING HUSBAND AND FATHER
X

Her Da's familiar "X" was at the bottom of
the page. Katy looked at the date that was on
the letter, it had been sent months ago. I wonder, she thought; before he left did he even
know that there was to be a new little one? Did

he even care she thought grimly?

There was no address. How could she tell him about their mother? He didn't even know they'd so recently buried her and that he now had a new daughter. They would not be able to reach him.

She fed Molly the rest of the bottle and re-settled her in the sling. Rising, with every bone in her body objecting, she continued on her way. With each step she wondered if it was really possible to make the entire journey or had she set out on a fool's errand.

By late afternoon, foot sore, back tired from the extra weight of the cradled baby, and trying to ignore the beginning rain, she walked off the road and into a nearby field. Tucked back through the grey drizzly mist, stood one lone barn. It looked dry and inviting if not a little shabby. Slowly, putting one tired foot in front of the other she made her way through the over-grown field and into the old stone building.

"Dinner," she said, letting herself in through the side door as she admired the cow who stood contentedly chewing her cud.

All she could think was to curl up in the warmth of the hay. But tired as she was she still needed to fill Molly's bottle to give her some little nourishment before she settled down for the night.

The old cow had been patient, not minding the gentleness of Katy's hands. She tried to give Molly small swallows of the fresh warm milk that she'd mixed with a bit of water hoping she wouldn't get sick on the rich diet. She had been so close to starving to death. It was good that she was satisfied with very little and soon fell into a deep sleep. The pitter-patter of the falling rain and the warmth of the hay felt protective and lulled them into a deep sleep.

"Hey you get up." She rubbed at her eyes and stared up at the grizzled face of an old man staring down at her, his shovel in hand ready to strike out.

"What..." she began.

"What are ye doin' here? Get on out of me barn and get off me land; get out of here 'fore I run ye through. Go on now. I don' want the likes o' you hang in' 'round here."

"But...," said Katy.

He grabbed at her; his grimy hand wrapped around her neck.

She stared into hateful eyes. Her mouth tried to scream but nothing came out. With one arm she held Molly protectively against her with the other she struck out, her fingers raking the side of his face.

"Why you," he said feeling the blood run down his cheek He shook her by the neck breaking the silver chain that held the locket. Katy, struggled to get free, her nails had ripped open his face.

He stopped, "What the..." Katy took that moment to twist free and was out the door before he even knew she was gone. She ran across the field leaping over rocks and tufts of grass, she could hear him bellowing behind her, and hear his booted feet pounding on the ground gaining on her. Leaping over the stone wall she ran, with a swiftness she didn't know she had, up the winding dirt road. Running as far and fast as she could, exhaustion overtook her, and she fell into a heap at the side of the road. With her last ounce of strength, she pulled herself up and crawled through the hedgerow and over the stone wall where she could hide.

Rain poured down soaking her, washing away the tears. Molly was getting wet, she had to find shelter. Searching through the grey mist she saw not too far away, a stone house long ago abandoned. Trying to ease the pain in her side, she chose her steps with care. It felt like hours but took only minutes to reach the shabby little house. Pushing open the door she nearly fell inside. Exhaustion overtaking her, she didn't bother to feed Molly again but curled up in the corner in a pile of dirty straw and went to sleep. Tomorrow they would get to the mountain.

· · · · · · · · · · · · · · THIRTEEN

Something was wrong. Katy knew it was more than the never-ending empty feeling in her belly. Her face was burning. The aches and pains were more than just from yesterday's sprinting to get away from the angered farmer. She wasn't feeling well and there was still at least a day of walking before she'd get up the mountain. That was if the weather held and if she could find the strength to do it.

There wasn't even a half-cup left for Molly of the fresh milk that she'd taken from the cow. If she could find water, she could thin it and maybe she could stretch it for the day. Easing herself up, dizziness washed over her threatening to topple her. This will not happen she said, I will not be sick. I will make it.

Moving with care, she pulled open the door. A hazy sun had risen high over the horizon, shining down on them. The warmth was a welcome treat. She knew they'd slept much too long.

With little thought she made her way down the untidy walk. Her foot squished something soft and mushy. She didn't even want to look to see what it was but then a sticky sweet smell filled the air. The scent was so familiar. How could this be she thought? Branches hanging over the walkway brought visions of home. A few apples still clung to the branches, shriveled but no doubt could still be eaten. Tears came to her eyes as she reached up for the once firm red fruits. Cradling Molly with one arm, she gathered an apron full then sat down in the sunshine and began to eat having no regard for the brown and mushy flesh.

"Ah Molly, we'll survive yet," she said savoring every mouthful. The juice dripped off her chin and ran down the front of her dress. "So fragrant," she said, "it's been so long..." But didn't finish her sentence, instead she took her time, enjoying every bite. When she'd had her fill she picked a half dozen more and put them in the sling with Molly. "This will get us there," she said to the sleeping babe.

It was close to noon when they made it back on the road. The mountain couldn't be more than an hour away. It wouldn't be long. And it wasn't that much further, although it took a bit to find a trail.

The afternoon wore on as she continued the upward climb, putting one foot in front of the other, at times hardly even aware of where she was. Her head throbbed, her throat sore. She followed the only path she could find, little used, but it led up the mountain.

In the distance she saw another traveler coming down the trail and though reluctant to stop him she didn't know how else to find her way. He was a grizzled old man bent over from the weight of a sack that must have contained a dead animal. He eyed her suspiciously as she spoke. "Sir," she said stepping aside to let him pass. Stopping, he shifted his bulky pack from one shoulder to the other.

"A good day to you," she started, "Do you know of a woman who lives up the mountain - alone?"

He snickered an unkind laugh and said, "Well I know of only one. No doubt you'd be thinkin' of the Widow." She nodded. "Ha, she's up there alright," he said jerking his thumb over his shoulder.

Katy didn't have the strength to question him further but stood a moment and watched as he continued down the path. She caught a glimpse of sheep's wool through the tear in the side of his sack before he disappeared around the next bend. If it had been stolen, she knew there was nothing she could do.

Footsore she continued to trudge up the steep side of the mountain, the winding path often difficult to follow. The sun was setting; a chill was coming with the night air. She took no notice. Still feverish, her arms blossomed with goosebumps. Another long hour went by. The falling darkness was almost complete as she curled up at the base of a huge craggy, moss covered rock. Snuggling Molly closer, she fell into a deep and troubled sleep.

Molly's crying and squirming woke her. It was morning; the sun was up but the rays were hidden behind the thick grey mist. Katy feared she would not be able to stand she was trembling so. Pushing herself up, her legs felt like warm oatmeal. Staring a moment into the greyness of the day, she tried to get her bearings. Molly needed something to eat or drink. The bottle was dry. She had two apples left. Patiently she chewed a bite of apple to a pulp and then slowly let it dribble into the lethargic baby's open mouth.

"We have to make it Molly, I promised

Mamai I'd care for you. We're almost there, I'm sure of it. It can't be much further." But a look of doubt clouded her eyes. She gave the quiet baby a bit more of the apple pulp then went to the creek that bubbled and gurgled on its way down the mountain. She filled the bottle with the clear cold water. Sitting on a nearby rock, she took a moment to soak her feet and then splash water on her face hoping it would revive her.

She had to get her wits about her or they wouldn't make it. "C'mon Molly," she said rising, her step unsteady, "We will find her." It sounded far more confident than she felt.

It must've been hours when she heard the bleating of sheep followed by the excited barking of a dog. It had been so long since she'd heard an animal that she stopped a moment and in her feverish haze wondered where she was and what it was she was hearing.

Peering into the half-light, she willed her eyes to focus. Not sure if it was her imagination or if she really saw something, there appeared to be a stone hut just ahead. Apple trees surrounded it like a protective hedge. There was a neat rock wall that enclosed a tidy yard. Was this real? Half delirious she stumbled towards the wooden gate, her legs threatening to crumple from beneath her.

"Hello the house," she said hardly above a whisper. Pushing the gate open she staggered like a drunken gypsy to the door. Unable to lift an arm to knock she leaned against the door-jamb and kicked out at the strong wood door. Her breathing was shallow, her eyes glazed over. Molly was perfectly still.

Something sniffed at her feet, a cold wet nose touched her hand and then the barking started. She heard scratching at the door.

A stern voice called out. "Rags, what in heaven's name is all the noise about?" The door swung open. The barking turned to a quiet whining.

"Rags..." the voice gasped.

"GrandMamai?" said Katy, her eyes unable to focus, the fever causing rivulets of sweat to trail down her back, her knees turning to mush.

A hand reached out to catch her as she began to crumple. "What is it you're calling me?" asked the tall vision at the door. With that Katy slowly slid down, fainting in a heap, her arms sheltering the still baby.

................FOURTEEN

Katy's eyes were closed in sleep. She was very warm and very comfortable. That much she was sure of. The mattress was the most luxurious she'd ever slept on. There were no pieces of hay sticking through, wanting to poke holes in her. A feather filled quilt was pulled up to her chin and her head laid on a soft down-filled pillow.

I don't want to open my eyes she thought. I'm quite sure I'm in heaven. Wherever I am I don't want this to end. She moved slightly feeling the whisper softness of the fine cotton gown rubbing as it glided over her skin. She inhaled the lovely fragrance of clean sheets, dried herbs and fresh baked bread.

A baby's cry pulled her out of her dream like state. "Molly," she said sitting up abruptly. A feeling of faintness and light-headedness made her fall back against the soft pillow. "Molly," she said again, "where are you?" She squinted her eyes looking up at the unfamiliar thatched roof.

"Well and it's about time you roused your-self."

Katy turned to the voice standing by the hearth. A tall regal looking woman stood with a long-handled spoon in one hand. The vision looked like a magic fairy queen holding a wand. Her back was ramrod straight. Katy looked closer. There was a familiarity about the woman. She could just make out the dark brown of her eyes and could clearly see the dark blonde bun with streaks of grey pulled tightly and pinned securely at the back of her neck. There wasn't a hair out of place. Her lips were pressed closed in a tight thin line. She had on a no nonsense crisp white blouse and a plain brown skirt.

"Well and can you speak?" asked the tidy vision standing at the hearth. Even from the distance across the room she could see the vivid color of the bricks surrounding the fireplace and the dullness of the stone hearth. It was different from what she had known – it didn't have the polished and smooth look that had been worn down by the many feet in search of warmth.

"Molly," she said. "Where's Molly, I need to find her," tears came to her eyes threatening to spill over. "I thought I heard her."

"Your baby is fine," said the older woman bending to stir the fragrant contents of the big iron pot, "but she almost wasn't," she added.

"She's not my baby," said Katy. "Where is she?"

"Right here," said the older woman, indicating a small cradle pulled up next to the hearth. Katy could see one small arm; fist tightly closed reaching up toward the roof, almost as if she were waving to her.

Katy, satisfied that all was well, could say no more and fell back into an exhausted sleep.

"Here now," said a voice sitting next to her, "You need to eat."

Katy's eyes flew open. Where was she? Her eyes travelled around the room. There was the older lady that she'd seen earlier, she was sitting on a stool next to her bed, bowl in her lap and spoon held high, half way between them.

"Have some," she said moving the spoon with the mouth-watering fragrant stew closer.

Katy, propped up by the soft goose down pillows, didn't need to be asked again. She took a tentative sip. She couldn't recall ever having anything quite so tasty.

"Finish this," said the tall tidy woman, "and rest a bit then I'll find a bite or two more for you."

Katy filled with questions sipped at the stew trying to not slurp and dripping only a few drops on the fine linen napkin that was spread like a bib across her chest.

"Alright now, rest and then we'll get more for you and maybe a piece of bread."

Katy, worn by the effort, laid back down falling asleep instantly, the stew warming her insides.

~

"You're going to sleep your life away," said the woman sitting at her side.

Katy opened her eyes and looked over at the woman. "Who are you?" she asked, her brows coming together trying to think or to remember.

"My name is Mrs. Kirk," she said looking down at the girl in the bed.

"GrandMamai?" said Katy her voice just above a whisper. It was more a statement then a question.

"You said that before," said the woman holding out a spoonful of more of the fragrant stew. "Why do you call me GrandMamai?" she asked a harshness creeping into her voice. "I am grandmother to no one. I have no grandchildren."

Katy reached up to her neck, her fingers

searching for the silver chain. "My locket," she said, her eyes filled with sadness as she looked at the older woman searching for some recognition.

"And what locket would that be?" she asked.

"I had a locket from my Mamai. It's gone. The farmer. He grabbed me," she said. "He tried to strangle me." She could still feel the fear and the ache in her neck where he'd tightened his fingers.

"A farmer grabbed you?" asked the woman curiosity getting the better of her.

"Aye, he thought I was stealing something. My locket broke when he tried to choke me."

The prim lady, her back as straight as an iron poker sat on the edge of the low stool looking at her oddly. A question in her eyes.

"Is Molly well?" asked Katy.

"She gets stronger every day," said the woman.

"And how long is it that I've been here?" asked Katy as she took in yet another spoonful of the fragrant stew.

"I believe 'tis near three weeks, might be closer to four actually."

"Oh no," said Katy throwing back the covers. "My brothers. I have to get back down to my brothers."

"What brothers? You mean there are more of you?" asked the woman, annoyance creeping into her voice. "And stay in that bed," she said, pulling the covers back over her. "You're not fit to go anywhere."

"My brothers are in the workhouse. I had to leave them there. They couldn't walk this far."

"And you could? Carrying a baby?" Her eyebrows went up as she spoke. Katy saw the color of her eyes. They were the same dark brown as her own.

"I had to," said Katy, "there was no other choice."

"What's happened down there?"

"You mean in the villages and the towns?" asked Katy, tired again just from the effort of talking and eating. She laid back down, cushioning her head on the wonderful pillow. "They're all starving to death," she said, "or they're sick. Many are dead. The potatoes rotted in the ground again this year - that is the few that people were able to put in."

"Humph," said the old woman, "That's too bad, you were about starved when you arrived here and I believe you had a case of the typhus."

"I'm sorry," she said. "Thank you for caring for us."

"You don't have to be sorry my girl. Far be it from me to ever close my door to a stranger. Now here finish up this stew and I have a piece of bread for you."

The two spoke little over the next few days. Katy staying awake for longer periods of time each day, but it was still exhausting to carry on more than the briefest conversation. And then after not too many more days, of good food and rest, she was able to shuffle over to the cradle and look in on Molly. When she peeked in to get a look at her sister, she was amazed and gasped in surprise. Molly remembered her instantly and waved her arms and cooed excitedly.

"Why look at you," she said. "You must be a changeling. Did the good fairies come and spirit my Molly away and leave you?" she questioned smiling down at the happy infant. Her now rosy cheeks had filled out like two just ripe apples. Her eyes were clear and crinkled up as she smiled at Katy. It was the first time she'd ever seen her smile. When Katy stood to walk back to bed Molly cried and would not be calmed.

"Alright," said Mrs. Kirk, "I'll tuck you in with your sister." Deftly she picked her up and brought her over to Katy as she climbed back into bed. "Here now," she said and tucked a soothed Molly next to her.

If she hadn't been so squirmy and curious she could've spent every night tucked in with Katy but with her new found energy and good health she wanted to be up on hands and knees and looking into all the curious corners. It made Katy laugh to watch her.

The days passed quietly as she continued on her road to recovery. Soon, after the weather had warmed a bit, Mrs. Kirk brought her outside to sit in the sun. Spreading a great quilt near her chair, she put the now almost pudgy Molly at her feet.

Katy could feel the hostility and coldness from her benefactor and was not anxious to cut off her generosity so had not called her Grand-Mamai again. Soon though she would have to leave to help her brothers. When she could walk the distance on her own, she would be on her way.

"Mrs. Kirk," she began on a day filled with the promise of a glorious fall, "I need to be getting back to my brothers. I'm feeling much better thanks to your care and I do believe I can walk the distance now to town."

"Well," huffed the older woman in her usual brisk and efficient manner. "How do you plan on carrying Molly? She's considerably larger then when you first arrived and she's not going to lie still in that sling that she arrived in."

"I can manage," she said stooping to pick up her now busy and curious sister. She certainly was heavier since they'd arrived nearly two months ago. Had it really been that long? That once tiny baby was now so happy and healthy and full of herself. She hardly sat still for a minute as if trying to catch up for all the lost time when she'd laid close to death's door.

"If you leave Molly with me, I will let you take the donkey, it will hasten your trip."

"Thank you GrandMamai ..." she started to say and corrected herself, "Mrs. Kirk" she said as she had been instructed. "But I would be afraid to bring a live animal to town. There's so much hunger, I wouldn't be able to protect him. When I left there were no animals, no sheep, no cows, no dogs not even a chicken. There is nothing left. If a farmer even has an animal now he keeps it hidden as best he can."

"Humph," she said, as though not believing the young girl. "Haven't been down off this mountain in years. No need to," she added, as if answering the question before it was asked.

Ignoring the explanation, Katy continued.

"In the end, we had to keep the last few chickens that we had inside our home, or they would have disappeared in the night. Mamai just closed her eyes to it," said Katy, remembering. A far-off look clouded her eyes. "Our last crop of potatoes, as small as it was, we had to grow in the yard instead of the field where we usually grew them. We were afraid they'd be dug up in the night."

"And did you not have a Da to watch out for you?" she asked as she picked at a lone piece of thorn snagged in her otherwise soft linen skirt.

"He went to America, he wanted to earn enough money to send us all tickets. I had a letter," she said, but she knew it'd been lost on her trip up the mountain.

"I must go. I will leave tomorrow," she said as she stood. It would be difficult to leave the comforts of the mountain home, but she'd lingered long enough.

. . . . FIFTEEN

"Good-bye," she said. "Good-bye sweet little Molly," she snuggled up to her one more time, inhaling the wonderful fragrance of the clean and gurgling baby. Bye, bye, waved Molly, happy to be in the arms of Mrs. Kirk, her Grand-Mamai. She would not talk about her past or let Katy talk about hers, nor would she allow Katy to call her GrandMamai. There was an unseen wall around her, one that didn't want to let anyone in.

"It shouldn't be more than a few days. I will find somewhere for them to go, or I'll bring them here," she said, her tone matter of fact. Her straight back spoke of a quiet confidence.

"All three of them?" asked the stately woman trying to maintain her composure but distracted by the baby's antics.

"Well and whoever wants to come, but we won't be staying long. We'll think of something. My brothers can work too. They'll fix that leaking thatch and bring in enough turf for your fire that will last all winter long. And if you'd like they can paint the walls too."

"Humph," she snorted. It was becoming one of her favorite words.

"Well goodbye then, and I thank you for the food," Katy said indicating the sack of bread and cheese and apples and the goatskin pouch filled with buttermilk. It had been safely strapped to her back. "You've given me far too much, but I thank you."

Katy hadn't seen that much food all at one time in over two years and it was a feast. And if all went well, she'd be giving most of it to her brothers.

"Goodbye Molly," she said again surprising herself by not wanting to leave the baby that had been practically hers since the day she was born. She turned quickly and headed down the path wiping impatiently at the tears caught in her dark lashes.

"Here now Rags," she said, "You shouldn't be so far from home." He wagged his tail in excitement, loving the attention from his new young friend. She reached down to pet his warm and shaggy head. He wouldn't be still and raced around in circles, his black and white coat glistening in the sun.

"Go on now," she said, "that's far enough, those sheep of yours will be in the next county if you don't hurry back." There were only half a dozen sheep to watch. There had been more than a dozen GrandMamai had said but one after another had disappeared. One had disappeared not too long ago, and Katy was sure she knew who had taken him but kept her silence.

The flock was important to her grandmother. She spun the wool into yarn, and she had mutton at many of her meals, thanks to the small herd. Rags well understood his duties but stood for a moment wagging his tail and watching her descend the steep path before turning back in the direction of his wooly charges.

The day was lovely, crisp and clear. As she wound her way down the mountain she searched in the distance for the town where she'd be going. It was barely visible, far off and difficult to see at such a distance. Only a few thin trails of smoke curled up into the blueness of the sky from the low chimneys. If luck was with her, it would only take two days, three at the most to get there.

It felt good to be wearing clean clothes without holes and without the elbows worn through.

She had on her GrandMamai's white linen blouse, a dark plaid skirt of a finely spun wool and a dark brown knit shawl. She even had on a pair of her GrandMamai's shoes, a nearly perfect fit with her long wool stockings. Her hair was freshly washed and neatly plaited in dark braids, streaks of blonde shining through. Everything would be fine now; she was sure of it. For a moment she stopped and turned to look back towards the peak. The hut with the trailing plume of smoke was hidden from view, but she knew it was there.

Night was closing in as she left the mountain trail. Little daylight was left. She would need to move quickly to find shelter that wasn't on the road. The mounting dark storm clouds were gathering on the horizon, but she took little notice.

Footsore and tired from the long trek she searched for an abandoned house where she could stay 'til morning. There were far too many. They had been abandoned either from death or from the people moving on, whichever, there was little left in any of them. She chose the one set back the furthest from the road, not wanting to bring any attention to herself. There would be no fire to keep her warm. Curled up in her blanket, she was asleep before the storm broke.

Setting out early she knew would be the better plan, but it wasn't to be. The cold sopping rain wouldn't let up. As the hours passed, it poured even more. She spent a long uncomfortable day in the damp hut listening to the rain dripping through the thatched roof. Puddles formed on the floor as the wet found each rotted hole in the thatch. There was nothing that could be done and so she spent another cold night wrapped in her blanket. In the morning, she would leave no matter how awful the weather; she knew she could not stay in the leaking hut another day. The chill had seeped into her bones, and she would risk discovery if she lit even a small fire.

Luck was with her and she set out just after light appeared on the horizon. It had started to clear and there was only a mist dancing through the air. By noon she was passing the farm where she had nearly been strangled. She walked quickly not wanting to be caught by that farmer again.

"I'll go back and look for my locket after I get the boys," she said out loud. "Then I can show it to my GrandMamai and she'll believe me that she's our grandmother." Another whole day was spent walking to reach the town with the workhouse. First the post office she thought. And sure enough, the same clerk was behind the window, with the same bored look when she asked for mail for the Mullaney's.

Barely even acknowledging her, he slowly made his way over to the alphabetized cubbyholes and much like a turtle in no particular rush went through the pile of M's.

"Mullaney did you say?"

"Aye." she answered, "Mrs. James Mullaney. Or perhaps it's just Mullaney"

"Well, there's only one here in the M's" he said, taking his time as he examined first the front then the back of the envelope. "Looks like it's come all the way from America. Well just imagine that."

This wasn't the time for idle chitchat. She snatched the letter out of his bony hand.

"No call for rudeness," he said, a scowl darkening an already angry face.

It was the same distinct printing as before. All capital letters. It was the writing of one who wasn't very skilled.

Having no need for further conversation and wanting to open it in private, she took her leave. The letter couldn't wait. She sat on the wide granite steps and slipped a finger under the flap; she was hesitant and not sure why. Eyeing the carefully penciled page she once again, said a quiet thank you to her Mamai for insisting she learn to read. Schooling in the farming district had always been sketchy, but her Mamai spent time whenever possible in teaching them all about the written word.

The letter started with *"DEAR MRS. MULLANEY."* Of course, she thought, how would anyone in America know she'd died months ago.

I REGRET TO BE WRITING TO YOU TO TELL OF YER HUSBUNDS PASSING. YER HUSBUND WAS A BRAVE AND HARDWORKER MAN. HIS LIFE ENDED IN NEW YORK WITH A ACCIDENT. I KNOW HIS WISH WAS FOR YOU TO COME TO AMERICA. HE BOT TWO TICKETS BEFORE HIS DEATH. HE WASN'T ABLE TO BUY MORE. THE TWO TICKETS ARE HERE WITH THIS LETTER. I AM SORRY YOU LOST YER MAN.

SIGNED, SAM

P.S. IT IS MY HOPE THAT THIS IS YER ADDRESS.

Tears clung to her lower lashes. What accident she asked herself? Who is Sam and was her father buried in New York and how would they ever know? Questions she was sure would never be answered. She couldn't think. Folding the letter carefully with the two tickets tucked safely inside she pushed it down deep in her apron pocket.

It was time to get over to her brothers. She'd worry about the rest of it later.

Her feet made little tap tapping sounds from the hard leather shoes as she walked over the rounded cobblestones.

The grey stone building loomed in front of her. It was just as she remembered, only if possible, it was shabbier and more run down than when she had last seen it. She couldn't remember quite so many windows broken or quite so many ragged people languishing about on the stairs.

Walking up the steps she looked neither to the right nor the left. A sadness crept into her, shaking her nearly to her bones as she made her way up to the grand doors. She slipped in with little notice. The moaning and sighing from the inmates echoed off the walls, it spoke of suffering and hardship.

Without asking directions she found her way up the stairs to the wards that held the men. Not wanting to enter the overcrowded and stinking areas, she peeked in, not sure how she'd find the three boys. Standing aside, she watched as two men walked out of one of the wards carrying an unmoving body that had no doubt taken its last breath.

"Katy?" A very small body slumped on the side against the wall, looked up at her, the eyes too big for one so young. "Is that you?" Staring at the hunched over shriveled body with rags hanging like old, tattered cobwebs, she didn't want to know this person. He coughed. It was a long hollow endless sound. She bent down next to the emaciated body.

"Conor?" she asked. She pushed the straggly hair back from the familiar forehead. "Is that you?"

Trying to be gentle on his small body, she patted his back trying to loosen whatever it was in his chest causing the coughing fit. She looked into the thin, drawn face streaked by tears. He was unable to talk, only able to throw his arms around her and bury his face in her shoulder. Grimy beyond description, with weeks of accumulated dirt, he was hard to recognize. Together they rocked back and forth, their tears mingling.

"We didn't think you were coming back," he said when he was able to speak. "We know how you've always wanted to go away."

"Oh Conor, it's not true. Of course, I was coming back. I've been sick."

He looked up at her, a terrible sadness in his eyes. "Eamon," he said, "he's gone." Katy looked at him, quiet tears couldn't be stopped. They slid silently down her cheeks and dripped from her chin.

"What?" she asked, not sure if she wanted an answer.

Conor, his shoulders slumped, his eyes not sure where to look stopped a moment. Just above a whisper, he said, "there was nothing to be done. He had the cholera. We brought him food. We stayed with him. We slept on the floor next to his bed. Sean stole food from the staff to feed him." This brought half a grim smile to his face. "Those sons-of-a-seacock stole it from the kitchen, so Sean stole it from them," he said in a very matter of fact tone. A smile wanted to break through with his pride in using curse words and not being corrected.

But he continued. "Katy, he was gone so quick," He swiped at the tears that wanted to blind him. "In the end he just kept asking for Mamai. I told him she was coming; it wouldn't be long. He'd quiet down some when I said that. He said his hand hurt too, so Sean bandaged it up again for him and told him it was going to be alright, Mamai would come and fix it." Quiet tears left trails through the grime on his cheeks.

Katy wrapped her arms around him and rocked him back and forth, whispering quiet words. It felt like a great hand had reached into her chest and was squeezing her heart. She was afraid it was going to burst.

The inmates of the workhouse had witnessed daily the anguish and grief of all the inhabitants and ignored them. It was easy enough to do, while the two sat holding each other.

"Conor," she was able to say, just above a whisper, "Come along we can sit outside. I have food." She didn't want to tell him that the stench was going to make her retch if she didn't get a breath of fresh air soon. With an arm around his middle, she helped her younger brother down the stairs, their steps slow and deliberate so's not to bring on another fit of coughing.

Settling in a sheltered corner away from the comings and goings of the residents and protected from the wind, they sat close together.

"And where's Sean?" She hadn't wanted to ask - maybe she didn't want to know.

"He's working," said Conor, "Splitting rocks a few miles away." He stopped and caught his breath. "I was too 'til some days ago - then the sickness took me." He spoke while he rubbed at his chest. "Can't go too far now. The cough gets me."

"Are there no medicines then?" she asked. He looked at her as though he wanted to laugh but decided not to and instead shook his head no.

"And will Sean be coming soon? We need to leave. We can't stay here."

"And where is it that we'll go?" he asked.

"We'll go to GrandMamai's. There are abandoned houses and barns all along the way. We'll be fine, just not here, not ever again."

"How will we eat?" His voice was raspy, and he tried to stifle a cough.

"I have more food and a blanket in my pack," she said patting the stuffed canvas sack slung over her shoulder.

"Don't take it out until we're well away from here," he warned eyeing the ragged group that surrounded them.

"Alright then we'll wait for Sean. Can you travel?" she asked. "Will you be able to walk?"

"Aye, I'm fine," he insisted. But she looked closely at him and knew that wasn't so.

. . . . SIXTEEN

Katy was sorry she hadn't taken the donkey that her GrandMamai had offered. Conor could've ridden him. He tried to keep up, tried not to complain. Katy walked on one side and Sean on the other; together they tried to hold him upright. They had been on the road for three days and still hadn't gotten near the path at the base of the mountain.

Katy had told Sean of the two tickets to America and instantly regretted it. He had wanted to leave immediately taking Conor with him.

"But Katy," he'd said, "we've got to get Conor on the boat then he'll be fine. He'll be able to rest the whole way over."

"Sean," she'd said, trying to move away from Conor so's he couldn't hear what she was saying. "Would you be knowing why they're calling them coffin ships?"

"But Katy..."

"Sean, I told you, I'd give you the two tickets on the promise that you'd wait for Conor to get better. He will get better if we can get him up to GrandMamai's. If we put him on a ship now, he'll not make it. Don't you know that?" Her voice started to rise. "Half the passengers die before they even set eyes on America. So, the answer is no!" She hadn't meant to sound so harsh.

"First we get him back to rights, then you two can leave." Hard to imagine she thought, first her father, then her Mamai, then Eamon and now her two other brothers were wanting to leave her.

"If you get to America," she said, "you find out what happened to Da, you hear."

"Aye, I know. I will," he said, kicking at a stone. "Da should have sent more tickets, then we all could go."

"And how could he have done that," she answered, bitterness sneaking into her answer.

"And then what of you?" he asked.

"There's no reason that I have for going to America." Her foot caught on a branch and for a moment she lost her footing. "Once it had been my plan..." she let her words trail off. Sadness was etched around her dark eyes. "I'll find a new home here; this is where I need to stay. Father always wanted to own land in America. It wasn't to be. Maybe somehow it will work out for me here. I'm going to own it for him." She hadn't meant to sound so downcast and added, "But Sean, surely you and Conor will one day have your own land."

"Aye, that we will. But not sure how you'll go about having your own land here. Women don't own land," he said.

"True enough, but I'll think of something," she said simply, her head high, her chin jutted out in a look of stubbornness. A look Sean recognized. It was that all too familiar look that she'd made up her mind and there was no changing it!

The dirt road took them past the all too familiar hedge. Katy shuddered remembering the farmer's grimy hands around her neck. Instinctively she reached up to finger the treasured locket forgetting for a moment that it was no longer there.

"Just a bit further," she said to Conor, her arm around his middle, his rib bones hard against her hand. "There's a small house up there, we can spend the night and get out of this rain."

Conor's face was hot against her arm, his skin a sickly white with two red blotches high up on his cheeks. "I need to go back to that farm," she said indicating what looked like an abandoned field. "I'm sure that's where I lost the locket."

"I should go with you," said Sean, his voice tired and strained.

"Nay," she said, "you need to look after Conor. It won't take me long."

They scrambled to get to the side of the road as the rumble of a farm cart came from behind them. They stood silently and watched as an old sway backed mule dragged one tired foot after another as he pulled the cart past them. The farmer, reins held loosely in one hand, tipped his hat in greeting. The three returned the greeting. Katy froze where she stood. Trying to get her wits about her she pulled a corner of her shawl up to cover her face.

"You," yelled the farmer, "you're the one," he shouted down at her. "Whoa," he yelled at the old mule. He pulled hard on the reins. "You did it."

"Run," she said to her brothers, "quick." She grabbed one side of Conor with Sean on the other and together they dragged their brother as they ran down the muddy road.

"I'll get you," he screamed, his voice cut through the air like the mythical banshee. "You just wait." She heard the creaking of the springs as he jumped down from the wagon. His feet pounded behind them through the mud, easily catching up to them.

"Run," she screamed at her brothers.

"You stole my cow." He reached out and grabbed one of her long braids. "I'll show you."

"No you won't," said Sean, putting up his fists, while trying to hang onto Conor.

In a flash the farmer raised the pitchfork he was holding. "Go on boy," he said, jabbing at the air, "I've got no quarrel with the likes o' you." His pitchfork, the light glistening off the sharp ends, danced through the air making threatening stabs at Sean. "Go on now get out o' here, she stole my cow. She's gonna pay."

"Run Sean. Get Conor to GrandMamai's. It's his only chance. I'll be alright." Sean turned; a look of agony hardened his eyes – Conor had slumped against him in a faint.

"I'll be back," he said, "And you had better not be around." A murderous look was in his eye as he dragged and tried to carry Conor down the road.

"I've got you now," said the farmer, his fingers dug into the flesh on her neck.

"Let me go," she croaked, his fingers tightened on her neck. "You have no right to hold me."

The farmer let go of her neck and twisting

her arm behind her back hissed in her ear, "Yer goin' to the magistrate's office girl, you can explain it all to him."

A dark sneer pulled down one side of his mouth. Katy recognized the three deep scratches that ran down one side of his face. They weren't healing well. Grabbing a frayed piece of rope, he wrapped it tightly around her wrists, the roughness cutting into her flesh. "There now, that should hold you for a bit."

He easily lifted her up into the wagon depositing her with a thump in the prickly hay. "We'll just keep you for the night and in the morning, it'd be my pleasure to bring you in to town," he said, a sneer twisted his mouth.

Trying not to whimper she struggled against the ropes, hoping to pull her hands free but he'd wound it so tightly there was no hope. Squirming to get comfortable, she leaned her back against the splintery side of the wagon. The roughness penetrated her clothes. Sitting still for a moment she listened. She could no longer hear Conor or Sean. With luck they were now far away. The drizzly cold rain fell in her eyes running down her cheeks. What was rain and what were tears was hard to tell.

The old mule pulled the cart into the

farmer's yard as the dark closed in around them. Katy was soaked through, the iciness raising goose bumps on her arms and legs. She was hungry and she was tired. Her only thought was to get dry and be curled up safely in her GrandMamai's soft and clean bed.

"In there," he said as he pushed her through the door into the dank interior of the stone house. Her nose wrinkled up from the smell. "Sit there," he said pushing her down to the floor. She sat on the hard packed dirt. The house was filthy. Perhaps he'd kept the cow in the barn, but the odor was so intense from chickens that had run free that she nearly gagged. No wonder Mamai shooed the chickens out, who could live like this?

The farmer mumbled words only he could hear as he poked at the turf fire. She watched as he loaded the iron kettle with bits and pieces of vegetables and a small bone, pieces of meat still clinging to it. Katy's mouth watered as the smell of the boiling pot filled the inside of the dark and dreary house.

Lacking the patience to let his meal fully cook, he poured the contents of the pot into a shallow bowl.

Her pride long gone she said, "Sir, may I

have a bit to eat?" Hunger made her stomach growl a low rumbling groan. His answer was the hard toe of his boot; it caught her in the fleshy part of her thigh making her gasp in pain.

"If I was wanting you to eat, I'd a given you somethin', now wouldn't I?" he said as he sat down and slurped one spoon after another of the hot soup.

Dribbles collected on the stubble of his unshaven chin. Tiring of spooning in the hot liquid he picked up the bowl and drank it down. Taking the bone in his hand, he chewed off every bit of gristle and meat, then threw it into the fire.

Watching with hooded eyes, she feigned sleep when he crossed the room and took a bottle with amber liquid off the shelf. His feet made shuffling noises as he returned to his chair. He took a long pull on the bottle. A line of dribble trickled out of the corner of his mouth.

"Don't suppose you'd be looking for this now would you?" he asked. The silver locket dangled from dirt-encrusted hands. His laughter was bitter as he watched it swing, the firelight glinting off the shiny surface.

"Found this I did, in the barn, day after you left. Don't s'pose you'd be knowing who it belongs to?" He laughed again then took a long gulping drink from the bottle. "Take it to town I will. Should bring me a few coins."

He sneered into the dark corner, his words becoming slurred. "Took my cow now didn't you. Thought you'd get away with it too." She pretended sleep. "My last cow, damn you. It's all I had left. They stole the other three. How'm I supposed to live?"

He took one long last swig on the bottle emptying it of its contents and then threw it. It shattered it into a million pieces. It was meant for her, but she was quick enough to duck. Glass splinters rained down on her. It was near impossible to feign sleep.

"I'll show you," he said starting to rise, but halfway up seemed to think better of it and lowered himself back to his seat.

A tiredness seemed to spread over him, like a fog that creeps in silently. The drink was taking its effect. Heavy eyelids slid down over unfocused eyes. "Take you to the Bailiff's, I will," he said, his speech slurred. His chin with its dribble of foodstuffs stuck in the stubble, sunk to his chest. His head slumped and settled on his arm resting on the table.

Hardly breathing, she listened as his snoring became deep and even.

Shards of glass were all around her. Sitting up straight, her hands tied behind her back, she let her fingers slide around in the dirt until they touched a sharp piece of glass. Ever so carefully she picked it up and holding it gingerly began sawing. There was a sting and then she felt the warm sticky fluid drip over her fingers when her makeshift saw missed its mark.

Ignoring the pain, she kept on with the sharp piece as she watched the snoring, drooling man with his head on the table. I can do it she kept saying to herself, visions of being arrested by the Bailiff danced in front of her eyes. She felt one of the ropes give way and quickly pulled her hand free ignoring the dripping blood.

Without a sound she rose, her eyes never leaving the drunken man with the locket still entwined in his grimy fingers. Somehow, she would have to untangle it. Then she could be on her way. Letting the light from the glowing embers guide her, she crept across the floor.

Reaching out she let one finger, then the next touch the silver necklace. Hardly breathing she unwound the chain twisted around his hand. He snored deeply, suddenly raising his head only to turn to a more comfortable position. She dared not move. His breathing became more even as she again tried to undo the tangle. First from one calloused finger then the other then the final loop hanging over his thumb.

It was free but now sat in a pile beneath his claw like hand. Thin fingers reached under the wrinkled flesh and trying to slow her heartbeat, she slid the silver locket out. Snatching it up she jumped as he suddenly lifted his head. With a great bellow his eyes tried to focus on her.

Stuffing the locket deep in her pocket she turned and sprinted to the door. Her fingers fumbled with the latch as she heard him rise up, his chair falling with a crash. The latch slid open, and she was out the door. He roared his displeasure as he lumbered through the door. Her foot caught on a stone protruding from the path. She went down. His hand surrounded her arm, tightening with a vise like grip. Not again she thought. Would she ever be free of this monster?

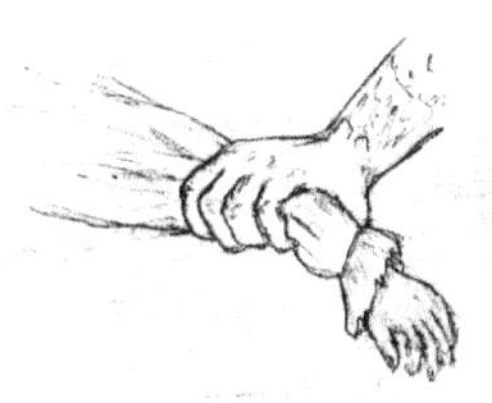

. . . . SEVENTEEN

Rough hands jerked her up out of the wagon; pieces of prickly straw clung to her skirt and stuck to her hair. He was a big man, and he was angry. One eye twitched while the other tried to focus. He had caught her when she tripped on the walk and in his drunken haze had thrown her in the wagon and lashed her wrists securely to the side. There would be no more escapes he said. She spent the night curled up in the prickly straw. He had risen before the sun was even up to drive her to the village.

Yanking her out of the wagon he cut her ties. "Don't you even be thinkin' of it," he said as if reading her mind. "There'll be no more escapes for you." He shoved her through the door of the huge building. It had a well-worn but official look.

"I didn't do it and you know it," she said to the leering face that glared down at her.

"Quiet girl or I'll be givin' you a what-for

'cross yer mouth."

She looked at the hard dark eyes with cruelness etched around the edges. There was no doubt he would do what he said. "Git in there now," he said giving her a shove.

"Got us a thief here," he said to the man sitting at the desk, who was busy flicking crumbs off his ill-fitting uniform. "Aye, is that so," he said, stifling a yawn. "Put her over there." With a jerk of his thumb, he pointed to the splintery wood bench. He yawned. "Tell me your name girl so's I can put it in the book," he dipped his pen in the black ink.

"But I haven't done anything," she said. "He's lying."

The farmer growled, his jowls shaking in agitation. He grabbed her arm and shook her. She winced in pain. "I told you...," he said.

"Alright now, no call for that," said the man behind the desk. "Sit her down and come back here and fill out the charges."

Katy, silent, tears from the pain and the humiliation, let herself be led to the bench.

"Come back in a couple of days," said the officer, "There'll be a hearing."

She sat in stony silence, the hard bench biting into her flesh. Her hand slipped into her apron pocket. It was gone.

A hand pulled at her arm. "This way dearie." A heavyset woman, aged beyond her years with thick black hairs protruding from her chin, stood next to her.

"But...," began Katy.

"Aye, I know dear, tweren't you that did it." She pulled at her arm leading her down a darkened stinking hall. "They all say that dearie."

Pulling a large key from the massive ring hanging on her belt she unlocked a huge wooden door. The hinges creaked and groaned as she pulled it open. They were met by an odor so foul it nearly choked them. Instinctively Katy threw her arm over her nose trying to cut out the smell. The old woman tittered, her prickly chin hairs quivering, "You'll get used to it dearie," she said. She led Katy past row upon row of cells, all with inmates moaning and groaning, all looking sick and half starved.

"Where is it that you are taking me?" she asked the old woman who had the vice like grip on her arm.

"You'll see dearie," her skeletal fingers searched the tangled ring of keys. Finding the right one she slipped it into the lock and swung the door open. "In you go," she said almost sweetly while giving Katy a hard shove. The metal door slammed hard behind her.

"What is the meaning of this?" She looked around at the sweaty, stinking, starving bodies. No one even raised an eyebrow out of curiosity so great was their misery.

Bodies were huddled against the wall, their knees drawn up close to their chests, but most laid curled up on the floor oblivious to whatever took place.

Katy's eyes traveled around the room as she stood statue like, fearing what she'd step on if she walked on the slimy floor. She waited a few minutes, her eyes adjusting to the dark. There were all manner of people and no room for her.

She was tired, her shoulders sagged, she just wanted to sit, but there was no room. Inching her way across the floor there was a small space to one side. She sank down, her back to the cold metal bars.

"Get out of there," said a voice that resembled a growl, "You can't sit there. That's where the food comes and it's my place, now get on with ya'." Slowly she rose and with great caution tiptoed between the bodies once actually stepping on something, a hand or a foot, she wasn't sure. A voice instantly lashed out at her screaming nasty words. She jumped back knocking into someone else who pushed her roughly. She'd disturbed nearly the entire cell full of bodies when a small patch of space opened up for her. Slowly she sank down to the floor.

"What's to become of us," she mumbled under her breath.

"Hee, hee, hee," giggled an old toothless hag sitting next to her, "we're all going to be hung in the morning for the thievin' scoundrels we be. Hee, hee, hee."

Katy gasped. "That can't be."

"Stop it you old witch," said a voice from the corner. "If you're lucky," said the same voice in the darkness, "we go to Australia, that's where they be sending all the thieves and murderers."

"But I didn't steal anything," she said into the darkness. She heard titters from some of the other bodies. "Neither did we," a few said and laughed a quiet mirthless laugh.

~

She lingered there for a week, maybe more, she wasn't sure. It was hard to keep up with days and nights in the darkness. She tried to keep track, but meals were served at odd times and there was no way to tell day from night in the dark and windowless cell.

On what must have been the eighth or maybe ninth day, the same rough woman that had called her "dearie" peered into the cell. "Kaitlyn Mullaney are you still here?" Katy gasped, not sure if she really heard her name. She shook her head trying to rid it of the fogginess. "Alright then. Guess not," said the voice in the darkness.

"What did you say?" squeaked Katy, her voice raspy from disuse.

"Kaitlyn Mullaney, I'm not asking again," said the heavy, big buxom woman.

"That's me," she said jumping up, her head woozy, threatening to pull her down from the sudden movement.

"Well then get over here dearie," she said rattling her keys as she undid the lock.

"And what is it you want with me?" she asked following the old woman who hobbled down the hall.

"Follow me dearie," was her only answer.

Katy stayed close behind down the long dark hall, her legs stiff with disuse. Coming into the office she had to shield her eyes from the brightness of the day that streamed through the windows. It was so welcoming but nearly blinding.

"Over there," she said. "You'll need to sit dearie."

Katy did as she was told, a thousand questions bubbled up. She sat on the hard bench where she'd sat a week ago and watched as one after another of the wretched, starved prisoners was brought into the room. A wide mahogany door was swung open and then closed as each body was let in or lead out, always in tears.

A neatly dressed man, his hair carefully parted down the middle came out "Kaitlyn Mullaney?"

"Here," she said. The color drained from her face, already pale to almost whiteness.

"This way." She rose and followed him into the room, wondering if there was a chance she could run and not get caught. The faded sign above the door had letters painted in tarnished gold leaf - COURTROOM.

"Sit," he said indicating the oak bench, darkened and worn with age.

It was too late. There was nowhere to run. Pushed down onto the bench a gasp escaped as she recognized the farmer sitting at the opposite side of the room.

"Alright, go on," said the man sitting behind the high desk. His wig was a bit askew and he was busy fidgeting with a wood gavel, turning it this way and that, admiring the brass adornments.

"Your Honor," said the farmer, "that girl stole my cow. That one over there." He pointed a grimy finger at her.

"What, Danny Kelly, makes you so sure she stole your cow?" He laid the gavel down, and focused a disinterested and tired look on the farmer.

"I caught her in my barn. I chased her out. She and that brat of hers."

"And what brat of hers are you referring to Danny Kelly?"

"There was a babe that she was carrying. I chased them out."

The man behind the high desk turned to Katy, "Why were you in Dan Kelly's barn?" he asked tiredly just barely able to stifle a yawn.

"We were cold, we were hungry, we were tired," she answered.

"So you sought shelter in his barn," he said more as a statement then a question. "And why is that a problem?" he asked turning back to the farmer.

"She stole my cow..."

"You've said that already. Explain yourself

please, and be warned, I don't have all day." His fingers returned to toying with the gavel.

"I chased her out, I did, her and that brat. But the little thief, she came back the next day and stole my cow."

"What do you have to say for yourself?" he asked, turning to the girl now standing before him.

"I didn't steal his cow. Why would I steal a cow? What would I do with a cow? I had nowhere to go."

"She stole it," said the farmer. "Look here," he said, fishing in his pocket, "I even have her locket, she dropped it when she came back to get the cow. See there's her likeness inside." The farmer moved closer to the judge to show him the likeness.

"Well then I've heard enough. It's been a long day already," he said, banging his gavel. "She took the cow and you've got the locket. Nevertheless, it was theft that got her the cow. You're sentenced along with the rest of this rabble to deportation to Australia."

"But Sir," she began. Her fingers were clenched into tight fists. Anger shot from her eyes.

"Stop," he said holding up a finally manicured hand, two gold rings shining dully on his fat fingers, "I won't hear it. Take her out of here."

Katy gasped then turned to the farmer, "that's mine. You have no right to keep it. Give it back." The farmer turned away and without a backwards glance, left the room.

"Guard," yelled the young clerk, his beady eyes looked over the tops of his spectacles. "Over here."

A surly, hunched over man answered the call. Limping to her side, he grabbed her arm, his grip vise like. Try as she might to wrench free from the iron grasp, it did no good. The grip only tightened. Dragged and pushed with the motely group that had already received their sentence, they were herded out, much like a bunch of cattle, through the waiting area. The crowd hadn't thinned. The room was teeming with people slumped in chairs, waiting their turn to be heard.

"Where are you taking me?" she asked the man holding her arm. She winced as he turned toward her; a grisly gash disfigured one side of his face; a black eye patch interrupted its route.

"Why to the cart of course along with the rest of 'em. Y'er all headed far across the sea," he sneered. She tried to look away, but his ugly countenance wouldn't allow it. His grip tightened as he shoved her forward, pain shot down her arm bringing tears of anger to her eyes. How could she contact her brothers or how to tell GrandMamai she wouldn't be back? How would they ever know what happened to her? Was this then her fate to be removed from her homeland forever?

. . . . .EIGHTEEN

Katy swiped at the tears with her sleeve. Hiccupping once she was not going to let them see the tears of anger and frustration. She turned to take one last look at the hall crowded with people. For a second only, she thought she caught a familiar sight. A gasp caught in her throat. She rubbed her eyes again on the sleeve of her dress. It was him! Sean was standing in the back, slumped against the wall, blending in with the crowd his finger raised to his lips to shush her.

The guard stared down at her with his one good eye wondering at her silence and sudden submission. Not wanting him to become suspicious she lowered her head, her eyes downcast hoping he wouldn't notice where she had been looking. "Get on with ya'," he said, giving her an extra shove.

They were loaded into an ancient wagon, one that should have been retired long ago. The guard moved swiftly down the line of scrawny, dirt-encrusted ankles firmly locking the chains connecting the group, one to another. There were twelve in all, men, women and two young boys. Hard to believe any of them had the strength to commit any crime.

With her chain clanking and rattling, Katy pushed her way to the back to sit next to the door. It was flimsy from age and misuse. The guard slammed it shut. It reverberated through the boards of the shabby wagon.

She heard the guard stomp his way to the front and felt the whole wagon creak and groan with protest with his additional weight. He settled himself on the seat already holding the driver.

"Git on with ya' now," he said speaking to the man holding the reins. "Should be no more'n two days most to the coast." The driver flicked his whip. The wagon lurched forward.

"Yep," said the driver, hardly interested in the conversation that the guard was eager to provide.

"If we stay ahead of the rain, we'll do jus' fine," he continued not concerned with the driver's lack of interest in whatever talk he was going to provide.

The wagon creaked and groaned in protest from the heavy load, "Can't you make them mules go any faster?"

"And how would I be doin' that?" asked the driver, his voice gravelly from disuse? "You got some suggestion as to how we can git a couple o' cranky old mules to go faster with a load like this?" As if privy to the conversation they swished their tails to be rid of an annoyance.

Katy heard him spit hugely over the side.

"Well, we're not going to make it at this pace and the dark is closin' in already. Me orders is to get this bunch a rabble to the ship by week's end and if you don't whip them mules into shape, we may not make it 'til next month."

"You wanna take over?" asked the driver, annoyance dripping from his words. It was hard to make out the guard's growled response.

Squinting up her eyes she peered out the back between the slats of the creaky door. There was little to see other than the falling darkness. If only she were free of her chains, it would maybe be easy to open the door and fall off the back of the wagon and then run as fast as she could. But her ankles were bound and as far as she could tell the only key was on the guard's waistband.

She looked at the other prisoners; there was little life in any of them. All resigned to their fate. Perhaps where they were going was better than what they were leaving. Yawning hugely, she tried to squirm into a comfortable spot. Rocking with the rhythm of the wagon, her eyes closed, and she dosed,

The doors crashed open pulling her out of a deep sleep. "C'mon ye' scum of the earth, out with ye' now."

A large greasy hand reached up and yanked her out the door and onto the ground. The others fell out or were dragged out, their chains clanking in protest.

"Over there," he spat shoving her in the direction of a small fire. She walked haltingly, her steps stiff with disuse "Sit," he yelled at them. The gash on the side of his face glowed white in the faded light.

The driver, ignoring the commotion continued stirring something bubbling in a small pot blackened from years of use. It didn't smell appetizing, but then most of them hadn't eaten in so long they didn't care if it was boiled shoe leather. The driver carefully ladled out two large bowls filling them to near overflowing. He handed the pot to the unshaven man shivering at the end of the chained group.

"Dinner," said the guard laughing to himself. The old man, having little care for how hot, gulped hugely from the pot and then gasping, passed it on. As it got closer to Katy it was obvious there would be little left. Sure enough, by the time it was her turn there were only drops at the bottom. She took her fingers and wiped down the sides, sucking in each drop that she could find.

"Gimme that pot," said the guard, his one good eye shooting sparks at her. He ripped it from her hands and threw it over to the driver. "Now get some sleep, we're leavin' early."

Katy, stomach growling with hunger, laid down where she was. Trying to squirm closer to the fire, the chain on her ankle halted her progress. Feigning sleep with hooded eyes she watched the two men. The driver walked back to the wagon and reached under the seat pulling out a small flask. Making himself comfortable by the warmth of the fire, he took a long slow chug, sparks of light glistened off the glass bottle.

"Give it here," demanded the guard, extending his greasy and hairy hand.

"Nay, git yer own," was the quick answer.

"Ya' best give it here," he said again, slipping

a knife out from the side of his boot. The blade flashed in the light from the fire.

"What're ye crazy?" asked the driver. The guard took a poke at him with the sharp point, a single drop of blood appeared on his arm. "Quit now, I was gonna share." Taking one more quick swallow he handed it over. The guard grinned, the only three teeth in his mouth gleaming menacingly in the light. In one long gulp he swallowed all that was left.

"Is that it?" he asked shaking the empty bottle.

The driver growled his answer and got up, moving away from the group. Katy listened to the cart groan as he hoisted himself up into the back and then settled himself down for the night. The wagon's ancient stays creaked through the darkness.

The guard growled curses under his breath as he curled himself into a ball close to the fire, his hands trying to find some warmth in his crotch. Katy, unable to keep her eyes open any longer let herself slip into a troubled sleep, too tired to care about the cold hard ground.

Something was pulling her arm - she'd been dreaming of sleeping in her GrandMamai's feather bed, dreaming of the comfort and warmth, but something was tugging at her. Maybe it was Rags, the dog, pulling at her, wanting her to run outside to play with him. She didn't want to open her eyes, somehow she knew that's not what she'd see.

Without moving she let her eyelids slide open. There was a shadow leaning over her. A familiar shadow she thought. A hand flew out and clapped itself over her mouth as a scream was threatening to erupt.

"Sean," she mouthed against the hand. She saw the silhouette nod. A barely audible sigh escaped with joy and relief. But how?

He moved away from her and crawled noiselessly across the ground towards the guard. Holding her breath, she watched in silent fascination as his hands, like feathers floating down, began to work with the key ring on the guard's leather belt. Secured only with a thin piece of leather, Sean, with little movement began to saw at the thong holding the key. The guard belched loudly interrupting his deep snoring. He shifted position then rolled back to the way he was. Sean sat back and waited for him to get comfortable again and to hear the rhythm of the drunken breathing of sleep. She watched as he released the key and pocketed the knife.

Creeping, without a sound he returned to her side. No words were spoken as he unlocked first her padlock, then silently went down the line unlocking others. One young boy woke as he felt Sean releasing his chain and instantly understood. Nodding to Sean he said nothing but took the key to continue on down the line.

Sean returned like a shadow and took her hand helping her up. With footsteps that made no sound, they disappeared into the night.

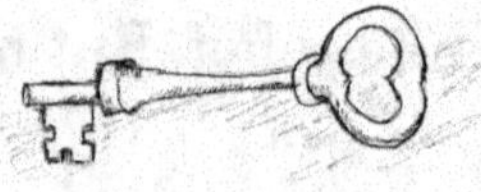

. . . . NINETEEN

"How did you find us?" She asked, her voice just above a whisper. They were far from camp, but she would take no chances.

"It was easy, those old mules that were pulling your wagon weren't going anywhere in a rush. I could walk faster than those old critters." She smiled. It felt so good. It'd been many weeks since there'd been any good news.

Walking down the road, they followed the light of the fading moon feeling safe and unchallenged yet still they whispered, always listening. Sean turned every few steps looking over his shoulder.

"I'm thinking if they find you Kaitlyn, they're going to hang you. Everyone is going to be looking for you, from the Bailiff to the Earl. They thought they were done with you when they put you on that wagon. This isn't going to go well."

"Aye, I was headed to Australia."

"And well I know. I was in the room for the whole thing. I heard most of what the Judge said."

"How did you get back here and where is Conor?" Her tone was hushed, she was sure she didn't want to know about Conor. Speaking it out loud would only make any grim news true.

"Katy, he was taken with the sickness. I got him to GrandMamaï's. He wasn't well."

"We're going to lose him too?" Her step slowed, her face turned up to the moon, letting it shine down on her.

"Aye, we may," he answered, "But I hid him and went to find where she lived."

"You found her?"

"Aye, and not so difficult either. There are few houses up on the mountain, and only one that was in the shade of a bunch of apple trees." She thought she could hear him grinning into the darkness with the pleasant memory.

"She came with me to get Conor and together we brought him up the mountain. She carried him most of the way."

"Does she know yet that she's our Grand-Mamai?"

"I tried to tell her, but she didn't seem to want to know who we are."

"But Sean she took Conor in to nurse him back to health."

"She didn't want to talk about it even though she looks at Molly and me a bit oddly now and again as though not quite sure. But Katy, there's more I need to tell you." He stopped and looked at her, his hands deep in his pockets. The air picked up bits of his thick sandy colored hair and twisted it in odd patterns. He hesitated as though not sure what to do but pulled one hand out of his pocket. "Katy, I have the locket."

She gasped maybe in horror or maybe in surprise, but she wanted to laugh. His hand closed tightly around it, a piece of the broken silver chain spilled out from between his fingers.

"All this and now you have the locket?" She wasn't sure whether to laugh out loud or sit down and cry.

"So, you see Katy, you cannot go back up that mountain. That farmer is going to think you not only stole his cow but that you came back and took the locket. He's going to raise a terrible row. He'll have everyone looking for you. Someone will recognize you for sure. There's nowhere that you could hide."

"Well, I most certainly can go wherever I like." Her chin lifted in defiance. "He knows I didn't steal his cow and how could I have stolen my own locket? Now hand it over and would it be too much to ask you to tell me just how you happen to have it?"

"Katy, I have it, what more do you need to know."

"Give it back to me this instant," she said, her hand grabbing at it.

"And if you're caught with it," he said, "what of the rest of the family? What if the Bailiff or even the Earl were to discover you? The Earl knows you took the lambs' bottle, surely his man told him. And what if he decides you took anything else that he happens to be missing?" He raised his eyebrows; a questioning look in his eyes.

"Then when the farmer hears you've escaped, he'll think you went back and got the locket and anything else that you might be wanting."

He tucked the silver treasure deep in his pocket, "And do you think for one minute they wouldn't take all of us in and maybe send us all to Australia?" His whispering turned into a hiss. "Are ye daft girl, that you don't see that?"

"How did you get it? The farmer had it in

the court."

"Now how do you think I got it? That farmer is a careless one."

"But I must go back. I've got to go to GrandMamai's. I must see to Molly."

"Molly's fine. In fact, she's better than she's ever been. She smiles and babbles the whole livelong day. There's nothing that we could do to make her life any better." His blue eyes had a hard edge. "If they come looking for you, they'll take her too. She'll end up in the poor house."

"I need to go back. I need to show Grand-Mamai the locket." But he was firm.

"I'll handle this," he said. "You don't want to get caught with it and our time here is limited." Without taking a breath he changed the subject. "You have two tickets to America do you not?"

"Aye, I still have them. No one took them. They look like pieces of paper, and no one can read."

"Well Kaitlyn Mullaney, I believe that's where we need to be going."

"Now who's daft?" she asked. With that the two almost as one, leaped over the stone wall at the side of the road as they both heard the clip clop of hooves coming all too close. Hardly daring to breath, they stayed perfectly still.

Kaitlyn reached out a hand and with no sound, parted the trailing greenery draped over the wall. They watched in silence as the guard, his eye patch black in the light of the moon, cursed and slapped at the rump of the mule. "Git on with you, you old bag of bones." They dared not move or even whisper until he was well away, and they could no longer hear his curses.

"Is this how you want to live?" he asked as they crept along one side of the road listening for other sounds and keeping watch for the breaking dawn.

"Nay Sean, I want to be free. I want to have my own place and not live in poverty ever again always wondering how we'll be getting our next meal."

He looked over at her, they were so similar, nearly the same height, with the same color hair. Only the eyes were different. "Then come with me to America. We can make it. It's only a few days walk to Cork; we can make it traveling at night. It's the only way."

"Sean, I can't. I thought I wanted to leave this country of starvation and hopelessness, but I know I can't. This is where I belong. I'm Irish and I always will be. My place is here. This is my country, I can't leave." She sighed. "My dream was to go. To start fresh. To get to America. But I can't. So, for now this is where I'll stay."

"You can't stay. You have to come with me," he said. 'We're no longer safe here. I will get the locket to GrandMamai. Conor and Molly are safe and well cared for. GrandMamai loves her already. We'll go and make our fortune and then you can return."

Katlyn looked over the vast rolling land bathed in the dawning light. Her eyes traveled over to the ragged mountains in all their beauty. She looked across the neatly divided fields their boundaries marked by the ever-present rock walls. How could she leave the place of her birth? But how could she stay? How could she be so selfish as to endanger what was left of her little family? Wasn't going to a new country what her father had wanted for them? To begin a new life in a new land? Isn't that what her mother would have wanted for them? And could they not return here someday?

"Aye Sean," she said into the clear morning air. "Perhaps you are right," her tone was thoughtful; she played with the end of her long braid, her fingers twining through the tangled ends. "Let me think," she said bringing an end to the discussion.

The horses overtook them before they even heard them. One moment they were alone on the road, the next she was thrown up on the horse and bouncing wildly. "Don't move or I'll cut yer throat," said whatever wild man held her down. Another horse galloped alongside.

"Couldn't catch him," said the other rider.

"Doesn't matter about him. Bailiff said git the girl. Well, we got her. And now we git to collect the reward." His laugh cut like a dull knife through the morning air.

Katy heard nothing else. Exhaustion had taken over. It was time to dismount. She was pulled off the horse. This is the end was all she could think.

"C'mon," said the one who had grabbed her off the road. "Bailiff has been lookin' for ya'."

. . . . TWENTY

He wasn't there. This wasn't the Bailiff's office. It was an abandoned farmhouse far out in the countryside. A holding jail they called it 'til they were either sent to court or as sometimes happened sent off to who knew where, never to be seen again. They left her, just like that. Locked her in what may once have been a busy farmhouse and off they went.

"There's a fine bounty we was told. We'll be getting' the Bailiff for ya'." Their laughter floated through the thick walls.

The day dawned so grey and rainy; she didn't want to move. Everything hurt. They had left her. For the entire day she moved around the locked space, trying to find a way out. The leaking thatched roof was too high to reach. There was no window and the lock on the door could not be broken. She had tried. Tried time and again, banging it with her fist and even kicking it. Nothing was going to release that lock except the man with the key.

They'd left her no food, only a small pitcher of fetid water that may have been sitting there for weeks. The hole in the thatch provided her only light. Would anyone ever return? Had they forgotten her? Winding her arms around her knees, she curled up in a ball and tried to sleep on the moldy pile of hay. Maybe when they found her, she'd just be a skeleton, long dead. It was hard not to give up. She had to go on, but how?

There were voices and the rattling of keys. She thought she was dreaming but then opened her eyes to see the door being pushed open. The guard stood staring down at her. "Out with ya'," he said. Where had he come from? But it didn't really matter.

Pushing herself up from the floor and putting one foot in front of the other she followed him the short distance to the room that held not only a fireplace with a warm turf blaze, but a small table. The Bailiff sat in a great chair. His hands folded in front of him.

"We meet again," he said. A smile played at the corners of his mouth. "I never lose my man," he said, "or in this case woman."

He strummed his fingers on the table. "Now this time girl, you have tried my patience and

I'm just about done with hunting you down. You're about as slippery as an old eel and you've pushed my good humor to the limits. This time we'll put you in chains with your very own guard." The burly man with the black patch looked at her, a smile revealed his nearly toothless mouth.

"Damon here is going to personally escort you to the ship bound for Australia. There'll be no more stealing cows, or lockets from farmers, or things from the Earl's estate, or whatever other mischief you've been up to."

"Do you have anything to say for yourself?" he asked.

She opened her mouth to speak, but the words caught in her throat. There was nothing she could say. She had no words left.

"Fine then," he said, his face almost amused.

A click sounded as the latch on the door to the outside was lifted. He watched with little interest as the door was pushed open. All eyes turned as a tall slender woman stepped inside. An earth-colored shawl was wrapped loosely around her shoulders. As she shook off the bit of dirt that wanted to stick to her skirt, her dark brown eyes took in the room and all those in it. She turned to the Bailiff. "A moment if you please." Her voice was soft, but strong and determined. "I have something to say."

"But…" began the Bailiff.

"No. It's my turn," she said, ignoring his attempt to interrupt. "I believe there's some discussion about a locket." Her stare would not release the Bailiff.

"Clifford, isn't it?" she said to him. He returned a barely discernable nod. "Weren't we in school together all those many years ago?"

The Bailiff shifted in his seat and began to fidget unable to look in the eyes of the woman standing in front of him. "It wasn't that long ago, was it?" she said. "Surely you remember."

"That I do Elizabeth Montgomery. Or Kirk now, isn't it?"

"It is to be sure Clifford, but my Colin passed away a bit ago."

"Heard you both had moved into the mountains years ago." Both spoke as if they were alone, forgetting there were others in the room.

"And that we did. We married and settled there not so long ago. Haven't been this way in many a year. No need to come down off the mountain that I know of 'cept, of course, when you're down here busy making mischief."

"But Elizabeth," he said, not wanting to

meet her eyes. "How can you say I'm making mischief? My job is to enforce the law."

"By scaring the stuffing out of a young innocent girl?"

"Danny Kelly said t'was her that stole the cow." He paused. "Danny said it was her for sure who broke into his house." He cleared his throat, "And then there's the Earl."

"Really Clifford? And do you not recall our younger years? When did we all start believing what Danny Kelly had to say about anything?" Her eyes would not leave him, "And the Earl?" she said. "I understand it's a matter of a tossed out bottle that once was used to feed the animals."

"Aye," he said still having trouble meeting her eyes. "What is your interest in this case, may I ask? What brings you down off the mountain?"

Her lips were in a thin tight line, but softness warmed her eyes as she nodded towards Katy. "This child who you think you are sending to Australia is in fact my granddaughter." Katy gasped. But the tall lady from the top of the mountain continued. Her eyes flashed for a moment as she spoke, focusing only on the Bailiff, ignoring the others in the room.

"I'll have you know she traveled almost fifty miles carrying her wee baby sister, trying to find me. She contracted typhus somewhere along the way and still kept coming. When she made it to the top of the mountain, she told me about the farmer's barn and how she'd gotten in, but it was only to get milk for the baby. She did not steal his cow," she paused. "Danny Kelly then kidnaped her."

"And 'Lizbet," he said, quickly catching himself in using a name that she hadn't heard in many a year. She raised an eyebrow.

"Yes," she said, "please continue."

"And why then," he said, "would you be thinking Danny Kelly kidnaped her?"

"It was against her will was it not?" declared the statuesque woman, giving the Bailiff a hard look with eyes that showed she would put up with no nonsense.

"And as for her breaking into the Earl's home, had anyone else seen this? Someone who doesn't spend his afternoons getting into a jug of poteen?" she asked.

She turned in the direction of the tall thin girl who so closely resembled her both in stature and bearing "I would like you to know that after she spent two months trying to get well enough, she set off back down the mountain to get her brothers who were in the workhouse."

Pausing a moment, she turned back to the Bailiff, "Her youngest brother had died, probably of cholera. Her other brother, who's just ten, was so ill, I had to come halfway down the mountain to tote him up to my home."

She took a deep breath. "Kaitlyn, along with her other brother Sean, had carried him from the workhouse. They were making their way to my home, until the farmer kidnaped her."

The Bailiff looked unsure, his eyes taking in all of her.

"Conor very nearly died on the way up the mountain."

Katy gasped behind her. Had he lived, she wondered, hoping beyond hope.

She continued. "The cholera was almost too much for one so young." Pausing a moment, she took a breath and continued. "Sean had to leave him in an abandoned hut while he came to find me. With his help, I carried him up to my home where he is now recovering and keeping an eye on his baby sister."

"Clifford, this girl is not a criminal. She's the daughter of my daughter. She's a strong young girl who deserves better than this for all of her determination through these dastardly times that we've all had to endure."

"She has done her best to keep her little family together." She stopped to take a breath and adjust her shawl. "Now," she continued, "I'd suggest that you stop tormenting her and let her go on about her business."

The Bailiff took a breath. "Can't do that Elizabeth. We still have a missing locket," he said looking down at his hands.

"Well, quite simply," she said, drawing herself up to her full height, "there is no missing locket. I have the locket. It never belonged to Danny Kelly. He stole it from my granddaughter." Her hand reached into her pocket. "Sean, Kaitlyn's brother, made sure that it was returned to its rightful owner."

"Here now," she said handing it to him, "if you'll open it, you'll notice that's my likeness from when I was a girl. You do of course remember my long braids." They exchanged a look and then in a voice meant only for him she added, "You certainly spent enough time pulling them."

This brought a half snicker from the guard. His black eyepatch wiggled up and down wanting to come undone from its tie. The Bailiff, red creeping up his cheeks, gave him a warning glance, quickly turning his smile into a frown.

"I also," she continued, "believe that my

initials should still be on the back. My husband had them engraved for my wedding." Turning the locket over, she allowed him one look. His thumb flipped it open, and he gazed down at the picture. At first glance it looked like Katy but now it was easy enough to see that he knew whose likeness was tucked inside.

"I see," he said squinting at the silver locket as he turned it back over. "E. M. K., for Elizabeth Montgomery Kirk."

"I have no choice," he said, "I'm going to dismiss this case." He banged his fist on the table much like he would've had he remembered to bring his gavel. "And Danny Kelly, will learn of this soon enough. You may go Kaitlyn Mullaney. I release you into the custody of your GrandMamai."

Pausing a moment, Katy's GrandMamai nodded to the Bailiff and very nearly smiled or as close as Katy had ever seen her smile. Putting her hand on the young girl's arm she steered her out of the dingy farmhouse.

"Come along," she said. Pausing a moment, another smile came close to lighting up her eyes. "You know, I too was a brown eyed child in a blue-eyed family. My parents were farmers in Germany. I married your grandfather because he was a weaver, and I could escape the farm." She paused a moment as memories flooded through her thoughts. "Then," she continued, "my daughter, your mother, wanted to run off with a farmer. I knew how hard the life would be. I had been the child of a farmer. I didn't want her to go through what I had gone through."

She paused, ignoring the tears that were collecting in the corners of her eyes. "I've had years to review what's happened in my life and the path I took. I'm not that sure that I had done the right thing."

Her eyes never left Katy, wanting but unable to see her thoughts. "I don't want you to go through the same life. You know it's going to be years before Ireland recovers. There's never been a famine like this." She let a great sigh escape.

"Your brother said that your father had sent two tickets. You may want to think about going to America and getting far away from all that's happened here."

"I cannot." Her answer came slowly, her eyes downcast. "It's been my dream all these years." She was hesitant to go on. Not sure if she was ready to say what she had been thinking while she had been locked in that dark and dreary room. "I'm quite sure that now I know. I'm Irish first and I'll not leave. Someday it will work out." She stopped, drew in a deep breath. "If America is still what I want when all this is over, I will get there somehow."

"But Katlyn, if you use that ticket it could be a whole new life, perhaps a prosperous life in a new country."

"Nay," she answered, brushing the wrinkles from the front of her skirt. "I think not. I think this is my home. I need to stay with Molly and care for her. Mamai would want me to."

"But child, you have the tickets. You have delivered your brother and sister safely to me. I will tend to Conor and Molly. There will be a boat leaving from Cork very soon. If you and Sean would like to go, I will keep the baby and Conor until you return. Perhaps you will find employment in the new country and then you could return when you've saved enough money. She paused a moment. "Or if you'd like, send for them later." Her voice trailed off as if she weren't sure of what she'd just said.

"Nay," said Kaitlyn, "The tickets are meant for Sean and Conor" Her determination was hard to miss. "They are both big enough to find some sort of work. I will stay here in Ireland."

Her voice trailed off. "Maybe someday I'll return to where we lived for Mamai's loom - if it's still there. Maybe linen can be woven and sold again and maybe the fabric could even be sent to America." An ever so faint smile wanted to spread up to her eyes. "For now, I'm quite sure my life is here. This is where I belong."

She paused, for just a moment doubt clouded her eyes. Straightening her back, she looked at the mountains before her and her gaze softened.

GrandMamai put her arm around the tall girl's shoulders, giving her a knowing squeeze. Together they walked towards the path that would lead them back up the mountain. Kaitlyn was on the way to her new home.

THE END

FACTOIDS

1. The potato arrived in Europe, by way of South America, in the late 1500s. It was introduced to both Ireland and the United States in the 1600s.

2. For the Irish, the potato quickly became a reliable food source. Nutritious and easy to grow, they were eaten at nearly every meal. An Irish man would often eat over 12 pounds of potatoes a day.

3. Most of the land in Ireland was owned by the English and Anglo-Irish. The Irish Catholics worked as tenant farmers, paying rent to the landowners.

4. The potato blight began in Ireland in 1845, lasting until 1852. The blight destroyed close to 75% of the potato crop, causing widespread famine and death.

5. A cure for the blight, Phytophthora infestans was not found until 1882. By that time, Ireland had lost nearly 25% of its population to death or emigration. A drop from which Ireland has not yet recovered.

6. Lack of support from the landowners may have been one of the more important causes in the failure to end the potato blight.

7. America sent corn (maize) to Ireland in an attempt to help the Irish. However, the Irish were not familiar with one of America's most prosperous crops and had difficulty turning it into eatable food.

8. More than one million of the Irish died during the famine from starvation and diseases such as typhus. Two million emigrated. Of those, more than half crossed the Atlantic to America by boat - boats that were often referred to as "coffin ships"!

9. Over one million Irish immigrants arrived on America's shores to escape the great famine. They were looked down on and signs were often seen where employment could be obtained: "Irish Need Not Apply."

10. There are many distinguished Americans of Irish descent, many with families who arrived during the famine years. President John F. Kennedy, Billy the Kid, Georgia O'Keefe, Walt Disney, Henry Ford, and President Barack Obama are a few of the many decedents of our Irish immigrants.

ABOUT THE AUTHOR

Tecla Emerson was raised and educated in New England, living in Lexington, Boston, Plymouth and Manchester-by-the-Sea. Currently living in Annapolis, Maryland, she is the author of nine young adult books and is the editor and publisher of *OutLook by the Bay*, a regional magazine.

She can be contacted at:
TeclaEmerson@gmail.com

Antietam
Waking the Fury

Emily at 15 is bored and annoyed with just about everything and everybody. Tired of her chores and irritated by the endless care of three younger sisters, she would like to have a life of her own. Her parents are absent; her father is off fighting a war she doesn't understand and her mother has left for Pennsylvania. As the eldest of the four sisters, she must take responsibility for her home and family. When the bloodiest battle of the Civil War is fought almost on her doorstep she is unwillingly pressed into service. Emily is called on to make decisions and to take charge of wounded soldiers while fending off the invading troops and protecting her younger sisters. Life changes forever as she discovers a courage that she did not know she possessed. Strengths emerge as she stands up for her beliefs while sheltering the enemy and caring for a runaway slave, both of which hold very serious consequences. In this remarkably accurate depiction of the Battle of Antietam, a legend is once more uncovered. It involves a mass of very angry bees. This dangerous, stinging swarm may well have had an influence on the outcome of that fateful day in 1862.

Jennie Wade:
A Girl from Gettysburg

It had been foolish to stay but now there was no choice. It was anyone's guess what the outcome would be. Nothing was as it should be. Oddly, the Confederate troops were pouring in from the north and Union troops were marching in from the south. They arrived in droves. The town was not prepared for what happened during the early days of that summer day in 1863. Jennie, a young local girl, did her best to keep up with the demand for bread and water and medical care for the troops. Her brothers were scattered, her sister would soon be having a baby, her mother was not bearing up well and Jack, her intended, had not been heard from in weeks. It was a time and place that would be recorded in American history forevermore. A time marked by the largest number of casualties in any battle during the Civil War. It was Gettysburg, Pennsylvania, a small, unremarkable town; an easily forgotten town that would live in infamy, and one that history would never forget. Of the almost 50,000 casualties of that encounter in early July, only one civilian was killed. This is her story. The story of Jennie Wade, a dedicated young woman thrown into the middle of one of Americans' most tragic times.

Mists of the Blue Ridge

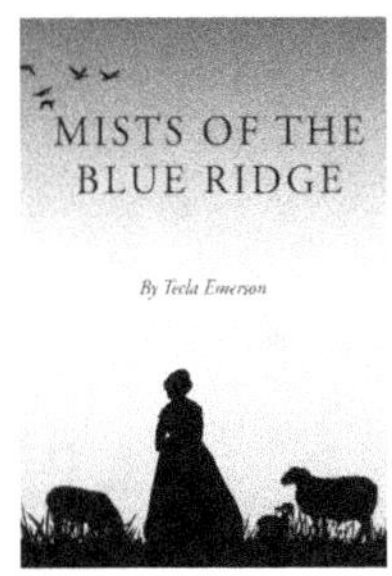

Olivia lived a quiet and protected life tucked away on a farm in the Blue Ridge Mountains. It was far from the great war that had been raging between the North and the South. She had little interest in the who and the why of it all and wasn't even sure where her sympathies lay. Then, without warning, the conflict surrounded her. At 16, she was ill prepared for the responsibilities that were thrust on her.

This is her story. It's a tale that tells of courage, determination, and survival during one of America's most trying times.

The Oregon Trail: Pathway to the West

Maddie knew the trip wouldn't be easy. Her mother and older brother were no longer with them and Hannah, her little sister, was hers alone to care for. And Hannah was mute. Mute for reasons no one knew.

It would take months to arrive at their destination. Months that would include accidents, floods, Indian attacks, and disease. The losses along the trail were both huge and unexpected. Would they ever reach the West, the land of their new home?

They traveled in covered wagons, on horseback and many times on foot. They risked all that they had, over the rough and not well-organized trails. It was a time filled with mystery and unknowns.

It would take months to arrive at their destination. Months that would include accidents, floods, Indian attacks, and disease. The losses along the trail were both huge and unexpected. Would they ever reach the West, the land of their new home?

It was 1845. A small group of daring and brave pioneers set out with high hopes and all their worldly goods to head for a new life. A new life in what was soon to become the Oregon Territory.

Shadows in the Fog:
A Block Island Tale

Molly lived on an island far from the mainland. She was an orphan and there was no one to care for her. Sent to live in a house filled with boys she was pressed into the role of cook and caretaker. Her life became that of a servant. When an unfortunate incident took place that threatened to scar her forever, she was sent to live with an angered and bitter veteran of the Civil War. Living the life of a recluse and with battle scars of his own, he keeps his past hidden from all. Hidden until Molly comes to stay. This is the tale of a young girl's quest for survival and how she brings herself out of the depths of despair as she learns of her mysterious past. Uplifting and compelling, the tale follows Molly as she matures and accepts all that life has given her.

Gift of the Winds:
A Tale of Hendricks Head Light

It was a lonely lighthouse, tucked far out on a Peninsula. Its function was to protect the ships at sea from the treacherous shoals of coastal Maine. Jacob and Sarah had done their job well all these years: keeping the lamp lit and sounding the warning horn whenever necessary. And now, unable to help, they watched as the violence of a late winter storm took out its fury on a helpless schooner. Sailing from distant Ireland, the ship held many of the Irish immigrants who were escaping from the lingering effects of the terrible devastation of the potato famine. Would there be survivors from this catastrophe? This is the tale still told today that surrounds that mysterious event.

Andersonville:
The Long Road Home

Hock snuck off in the dark of night to join the Union Army. He was too young to be part of the fighting force – but now, taller than most, he easily joined their ranks. Wounded in the battle at Petersburg he was captured and sent to a Confederate prisoner-of-war camp – a camp so horrid, it is still written of today. As one more of Andersonville's nameless inmates, he was given a number. Identified as "Unknown 9586," he was thrown on the death cart and hauled out as one of the dead.

"Unknown 9586," did not rest in peace. Leaving the site of his burial, he set out for the north. Alone, starving, wounded and unarmed he began his journey. This is his story. From the hills of Vermont to the sights and scenes of horror that are found on battlefields and then to his final destination. It's the tale of prisoner #9586 – Unknown. The prisoner who missed his own burial.

www.ingramcontent.com/pod-product-compliance
Lightning Source LLC
Chambersburg PA
CBHW070342200726
48294CB00003B/754